~ DREAM ~

JENNY COLGAN

Praise for Jenny Colgan

'I love this book! It's funny, page-turning
and addictive . . . just like Malory
Towers for grown-ups'

Sophie Kinsella

'I have been waiting twenty-five years for someone
to write a bloody brilliant boarding school
book, stuffed full of unforgettable characters,
thrilling adventures and angst and here it is'

Lisa Jewell

'A wonderful first novel that had me in tears
and fits of laughter. Definitely an A*!'

Chris Manby

'If you were a fan of Malory Towers
or St Clare's books in your – ahem –
youth, you'll love this modern boarding
school-based tale . . . Top of the class!'

Closer (four-star review)

'This brilliant boarding school book, with its eccentric cast of characters and witty one-liners, should prove an unmissable dose of nostalgia. Whether you've recently left school, have rose-tinted memories of it or are a teacher looking for some escapism from classroom dreariness, this book will certainly score A*'

Glamour

'Good old-fashioned fun and escapism . . . A fabulously fresh and fun read'

Heat (four-star review)

'This is Malory Towers . . . for grown-ups'

Company

'If you're looking for delightful childhood reminiscing or perhaps are the person who fantasised about being in a boarding school as a youngster, then this is the book for you!'

BookPleasures.com

Jenny Colgan is the author of numerous bestselling novels, including *The Little Shop of Happy Ever After* and *Summer at the Little Beach Street Bakery*, which are also published by Sphere. *Meet Me at the Cupcake Café* won the 2012 Melissa Nathan Award for Comedy Romance and was a *Sunday Times* top ten bestseller, as was *Welcome to Rosie Hopkins' Sweetshop of Dreams*, which won the RNA Romantic Novel of the Year Award 2013. Jenny was born in Scotland and has lived in London, the Netherlands, the US and France. She eventually settled on the wettest of all of these places, and currently lives just north of Edinburgh with her husband Andrew, her dog Nevil Shute and her three children: Wallace, who is fourteen and likes pretending to be nineteen and not knowing what this embarrassing 'family' thing is that keeps following him about, Michael-Francis, who is twelve and likes making new friends on aeroplanes; and Delphine who is ten and is mostly raccoon as far as we can tell so far.

Things Jenny likes include: cakes; far too much Doctor Who; wearing Converse trainers every day so her feet are now just gigantic big flat pans; baths only slightly cooler than the surface of the sun, and very, very long books, the longer the better. For more about Jenny, visit her website and her Facebook page, or follow her on Twitter @jennycolgan.

JENNY COLGAN

Lessons

Third Year at Downey House

sphere

SPHERE

First published in Great Britain in 2019 by Sphere
This paperback published in Great Britain in 2020 by Sphere

1 3 5 7 9 10 8 6 4 2

Typeset in Palatino by M Rules
Printed and bound in Great Britain by Clays Ltd, Elcograf S.p.A.

Papers used by Sphere are from well-managed forests
and other responsible sources.

MIX
Paper from
responsible sources
FSC® C104740

Sphere
An imprint of
Little, Brown Book Group
Carmelite House
50 Victoria Embankment
London EC4Y 0DZ

An Hachette UK Company
www.hachette.co.uk

www.littlebrown.co.uk

To librarians.
Because you built me.

Introduction

Woah. So, anyway, here is sequel to a book I wrote *ten years ago*. I know. This is so weird, I never quite thought we'd get here.

To those who kept the faith: thank you. You should know that we are picking up again five seconds after we left off, even though when we left off there was no such thing as Facebook or Snapchat ... sigh. I miss those days.

Anyway, if you're new, I would probably read *Class* and *Rules* first, which cover the first and second years. My publisher will kill me for saying that, but honestly, they're meant to be read in sequence, and this is the third year of Downey House.

Here's just to recap the history a bit:

A few years ago I wanted to read a boarding school book, having loved them when I was younger. But I couldn't find one for grown-ups. So I wrote a couple.

We then decided ('we' being me and my publishers) to release them under a different name, Jane Beaton. I can't remember why now. It *seemed* like a good idea at the time.

Anyway, regardless, *Class* and *Rules* came out and they had lovely reviews but as it turned out absolutely nobody bought them at all, having never heard of Jane Beaton, which was perfectly understandable, but also made me very sad as I had loved writing them and was very proud of them.

As the years have gone on, though, people kept finding their way to them, little by little – they've never been out of print – and finally last year somebody wrote the publishers a letter saying 'do please let me know what happened to Jane Beaton, as I kept checking the obituaries in case she died' and someone else wrote and said, 'I'm going in for an operation and in case I don't come round*, I would very much like to know what happens to Maggie and David,' at which point we thought, okay, *enough is enough* – and so we reissued the first two, *Class* and *Rules*, last year, and now here is *Lessons*, the brand-new one, and hopefully now I'll get to finish all six and we will end up with a slipcase, which is pretty much all I dreamed of all along.

Very warmest wishes,

Jenny

x x x

---

* They were fine! It's okay!

Characters

Staff

Headteacher: Dr Veronica Deveral
Head of English: Miss June Starling
Matron: Miss Doreen Redmond
Cook: Mrs Joan Rhys
Caretaker: Mr Harold Carruthers

Physics: Mr John Bart
Music: Mrs Theodora Offili
French: Mademoiselle Claire Crozier
English: Miss Margaret Adair
IT: Mrs Margia Radzicki
Maths: Miss Ella Beresford
PE: Miss Janie James
Drama: Miss Fleur Parsley
History: Miss Catherine Kellen
Geography: Miss Deirdre Gifford

Pupils

Middle School Year Three

Sylvie Brown
Ismé Elgar-Phipps
Imogen Fairlie
Simone Pribetich
Andrea McCann
Felicity Prosser
Zazie Saurisse
Alice Trebizon-Woods
Astrid Ulverton

AUTUMN

Chapter One

Despite the summer sun outside, it was freezing in the long, dim hallway, and Maggie Adair was having the very worst day of her life.

It was the last day of the summer term.

The girls had all left, and the entire ancient, rambling building, with its four towers, was silent. The beautiful grey-stoned space did not suit being silent; it normally echoed to the sound of footfalls; girls shouting out; giggling and bells; rogue hockey balls bouncing down the old steps; distant choir practice.

All of that had gone, and the panelled hallway, hung with portraits of headmistresses past, was silent and ghostly. Maggie shivered.

Had it really only been that morning? How? How had she gone from getting on a train, on her way to Scotland to marry ... Oh my God. Stan. Her sweet fiancé Stan, who would be waiting to meet her at the other end.

She sent off a text that just said, *Missed train! Too expensive to get next one, will catch tomorrow!* then quickly bundled her phone away and refused to look at it, even when it started buzzing and buzzing. She couldn't ... She had too many things to think about right now.

She tried to get it straight in her head.

She'd caught the train this morning as she'd always planned. The school year was over and she was heading back to Scotland for the holidays.

On the train she had met Miranda, the ex-girlfriend of David McDonald, the English teacher at Downey boys' school, just over the hill. The man on whom ... she'd had a crush. It sounded so ridiculous when she thought about it like that; just exactly like the schoolgirls she dealt with every day on Charlie Puth or Alfie Deyes or whoever it was this week.

But it had been more than that. Hadn't it? Even though in two years they had shared just one kiss. That was all. And she couldn't even think about that without a blush starting. But she had put it behind her. For Stan, and the long years they'd spent together.

And then. And then ...

Oh my God. What had happened? Just as the train had been pulling out, David had vaulted the barrier and started running towards the carriage she and Miranda were sitting in.

And in a split second that had changed – and potentially ruined – her life for ever, she had reached up, slowly, almost as if her hand was under someone else's control – and pulled the emergency cord.

Chapter Two

The entire train had staggered. An old lady had fallen over, which Maggie felt absolutely awful about. She had rushed to her aid, but the lady had flapped her away. A lot of other people appeared to be swearing at her. There was shouting and consternation, and it had lasted a long time. Meanwhile, Miranda was leaning out of the open window screeching, 'David! David!'

But neither of them got to see him. As soon as he'd vaulted the barriers, an alarm had gone off, and the police who patrolled even Devon railway stations these days had tackled him, sending him sprawling to the floor, then handcuffed him and bundled him away at the speed of light, Maggie craning her neck to catch a glimpse of him.

The next second, the train was besieged with railway staff, Miranda had somehow disappeared and Maggie found herself completely alone, standing next to the cord, waiting as a very angry-looking guard bore down on her.

After bundling her into a little room off the main concourse to give her an extremely stern talking-to about whether she realised that everyone had thought they were going to blow up the train, and how she absolutely couldn't behave like that, and how she'd thrown off the entire network, and how the fine might just be the start of it, Maggie had broken down in sobs, completely, and they'd asked if they could phone someone on her behalf, but it couldn't be David, of course, and oh God, how could she possibly explain this to Stan, and everyone else had dispersed for the summer, which was why they had eventually got in touch with Dr Deveral, the head-mistress of Downey House, and why she had been deposited by the British Transport Police back where this had all started.

It was hard to believe it was barely lunchtime.

In the corridor, she buried her face in her hands. She had never felt more alone. She was a grown woman, engaged to be married, who had embarked on a flirtation . . .

No. That didn't sound right. That wasn't what she had had with David, not at all. It wasn't some grubby Facebook affair; it had been more than that. Something deeper and more serious. She tried not to picture him: those dark eyes with their long lashes; that grin that came and went at unexpected moments; his long frame striding across the hills with his dog Stephen Dedalus . . .

A crush, that was what she'd had, she told herself firmly again. A crush like half of the upper fourth also had on him, desperate for glimpses when the classes got together for drama or concerts. She had a deep, passionate crush on a teacher. Not something that had happened to her when she was at school; something that had waited until she was grown up and a teacher herself. She was just a late devel-oper, that was all. And what did she tell her girls when they got helpless, passionate crushes on pop stars or YouTube stars? It's normal, it's part of growing up, it will pass and help you to form real adult relationships; proper ones with proper adults with genuine flaws and complexities who see you as you are, rather than an unrealistic, idealised state of romance . . .

6

But still, how could she help what she was feeling? And what she was feeling was so very, very strong. It hadn't dampened down, hadn't settled at all. She had thought of him every second that summer term, wondering what he was doing; every sleepless night, twisted in the bedclothes of her single bed in her turret rooms.

And he had come for her. Hadn't he? Or was it for Miranda? She didn't even know. Her phone was buzzing buzzing buzzing – but not from him.

Oh God. A wedding planned. Invitations sent. Stan waiting after she had sworn to him, sworn to his face on the lives of her beloved nephews Cody and Dylan, that this was it, that she would never, ever get caught up with David again. A dress hanging on the back of a door.

Her stomach was ice water. How had everything gone so wrong? This was such a mess.

Chapter Three

'Wallet, keys ... '

The policeman looked askance at David's keys as he filled in the discharge form; they were ancient, heavy things.

'Where do you live, a dungeon?'

David tried to smile, but couldn't. Dr Fitzroy, his headmaster, was waiting right outside. This wasn't going to be remotely pleasant.

'A school, for now ... '

The policeman looked up at him, narrowing his eyes, then shook his head as he ticked off the list.

'Right, that's your lot.'

David blinked.

'And my phone?' he said.

The policeman looked in the bag.

'No phone here.'

David cursed. He hated his mobile phone at the best of times. But the one thing it did have was absolutely the only thing he needed: Maggie's number. If they couldn't find it, what would he do? If he couldn't get in touch with her ... couldn't call her ... He had to explain.

But then surely, now, that would be the last thing she would want. He thought of her face, staring blankly at him even as Miranda was screaming something. He still didn't know who had pulled the emergency cord, still didn't know who had caused the ruckus; it had all been so fast, so confusing, and he had, as usual, ruined everything – absolutely everything – with his idiocy. What had he been thinking?

'Oh, you're right, here it is,' said the policeman, pulling something from underneath the counter. 'Sorry about that. It's such an old model, I don't think the young plod realised what it was, to be honest.'

He looked at it.

'Can you get, like, the internet on that?'

'No,' said David, staring at it.

'It's amazing it still works.'

Now that he was leaving, the policeman was positively chatty; rather a contrast to how everything had been just a few hours before.

'Right,' he said, sliding some pieces of paper across for David to sign. 'It's up to Network Rail whether they charge you or not.'

'I realise that,' said David.

The policeman shook his head.

'For a lady, right?'

David winced.

'Well,' said the man. 'I've been married twenty-eight years, and I tell you, they all look the same after a bit.'

There was a very long pause at that. Finally, 'Can I go?' said David.

'Oh yeah, right, fine,' said the policeman, pressing the button on the wall that buzzed open the heavy door. Dr Fitzroy was standing there, wearing a facial expression the pupils of Downey Boys had long learned to dread: irritation mixed with profound disappointment.

'Mr McDonald,' he said solemnly.

The ride back to school was completely silent and very, very long. Dr Fitzroy didn't speak at all, merely heaved a sigh from time to time. Meanwhile David picked up his phone, wondering what the hell there was to say, then put it down again.

Maggie was getting married. This entire thing, the grand gesture ... He was a fool. An utterly ridiculous fool.

The boys had all left now, the last coaches just departing and the sun getting lower in the sky. It seemed incredible to David that it was the same day; that he had awoken that morning so sad, then suddenly so full of a ridiculous, crazy hope. And now ...

Dr Fitzroy told him abruptly to get changed and report to his office.

'I don't know if they're going to press charges ... ' David had started.

'They are' said Dr Fitzroy shortly. 'They called the school and left a message.'

'Oh,' said David, his heart sinking even further.

They entered the headmaster's office. In contrast to the clear grey stone and four turrets of Downey House, Downey Boys was of a later vintage: Victorian, and built with many curlicues and bits and pieces of ornamentation all around. The head's study was entirely wood-panelled, and much of the original Victorian furniture remained. The view from the many small windows was straight down the valley, to where Downey House could just be spied, nestling in the headlands a mile or so away.

Dr Fitzroy waited until the heavy oak door had finally shut behind them. Then he turned round.

'What the *hell* were you thinking?' he shouted in a voice he rarely used but which could make the windows rattle. David flinched, feeling more like one of the pupils than a teacher of many years' standing.

10

'I wasn't,' he muttered, looking far younger than his thirty-four years.

'Have you any idea how difficult it is to find good male English teachers? Who can handle a class and inspire their pupils? For Christ's sake, David, you were one of the good guys. You know I had you in line for head of department?'

David swallowed. He had resisted all attempts to put him in a more administrative role, but now wasn't the time to mention it.

'So . . .' he began.

'You'll have a conviction!' shouted Dr Fitzroy. 'I don't think you understand what's going on here.'

It was true. Until that instant, all his thoughts had been of Maggie. It hadn't even occurred to him.

'I'm going to lose my job?' he said, going white suddenly. It couldn't be more than a misdemeanour, surely.

'You'll have a conviction!' said Dr Fitzroy. 'You have to see I have absolutely no choice in the matter.'

'For trespassing in a railway station?' said David. 'I mean, surely it's not that—'

'It's a prevention-of-terrorism offence!' said Dr Fitzroy.

'Oh,' said David, startled.

'You're lucky you weren't shot.'

'I'm so sorry, sir.'

'Yes, well. Bit late for that,' said the headmaster. 'Just as well it's the end of term.'

They sat in silence. David felt an utter failure. He had brought this on himself. Of course he had.

He looked out at the old buildings, through the window with its beautiful view of the sparkling sea, promising a glorious summer ahead.

'I'm so sorry I let you down, sir.'

'You've let everybody down,' said the headmaster. 'Me,

the boys ... yourself most of all. You had a perfectly nice fiancée, as far as I remember. Why not just marry her instead of getting up to these ridiculous tricks? With another teacher! Veronica is in a worse state than I am.'

David couldn't imagine the cool Dr Deveral remotely flustered about anything, but he didn't feel it was the time to say that. He stood up slowly. He'd have to go and pack.

Chapter Four

On the other side of the hill, Maggie was also staring at the floor. Veronica Deveral, the cool, fair headmistress of Downey House, had left her sitting for a long time outside her office; partly to give Maggie time to calm down and hopefully stop crying – Veronica was not a fan of tears – and partly to give herself time to decide what to do. She'd already spoken to Robert Fitzroy at Downey Boys; he was just as aghast as she was, and she knew David wasn't going to keep his job.

She'd resigned herself to losing Maggie after she got married; was sure she'd return to Scotland. Now it looked like a chink of light. Maggie was the best English teacher she had – impulsive, but utterly committed to her students. Veronica had absolutely no wish to spend all summer recruiting; Robert already sounded wildly disgruntled. It was just possible she could scare Maggie straight.

She summoned her. Maggie shuffled in, trying to remind herself how much Dr Deveral hated tears (which wasn't a particularly useful way to stop them).

'Miss Adair, this is a boarding school. This is the girls' *home*. Parents trust us not just with the mental education of their children, but with their moral education too. They entrust their precious, precious children to us; surrender them absolutely.'

Maggie nodded, biting her lip. She knew Dr Deveral was

right. It had been the heat of the moment. It had been a ridiculous thing to do, something she'd realised the instant the train had screeched to a halt.

'I can't . . . I mean, I'm sorry.'

'Fraternisation between the schools . . . it's not normally a staff problem.'

'No.'

'I mean, if the teachers can't keep apart, who's to say we won't be sending their sixteen-year-olds home pregnant?'

Maggie's face flamed. Dr Deveral made her feel like a teenager at the best of times, and these were patently not the best of times.

'Are you an item? A serious item?'

Maggie shook her head. Dr Deveral sighed.

'I thought you were getting married to that Scottish boy?'

I won't cry, said Maggie to herself. I won't cry. I won't.

'Stop crying,' said Veronica, who genuinely couldn't bear it. She pushed over the box of tissues she kept on her desk in any case.

'You can't fraternise here. Do you understand? It's spelled out very clearly in your terms of service. Not if you want to keep your job. It's a bad example for the girls; it's absolutely suicidal with the parents. I mean, this is going to be in the papers, you know that?'

Maggie hung her head, utterly humiliated.

'Are you going to let me go?'

Veronica sat back in her seat and looked at her carefully.

'Well. That very much depends.'

'I'm sorry you have to go,' said Dr Fitzroy gruffly. 'At least until it all dies down.'

David nodded. 'I am genuinely sorry to put you to so much trouble.'

14

'It *is* trouble,' said Dr Fitzroy. 'I'll need to find a replacement.'

'I'm happy to keep helping the Ks.'

K class were those who had trouble keeping up. David dedicated vast amounts of time to coaching them gently to a basic standard.

'No, you don't understand. You won't be allowed on to school property at all until all of this calms down. It will be in the paper! I can only imagine what the parents will make of it. I'll need to write to them all.'

David bowed his head. He wasn't contrite for himself, but he hated reflecting badly on the school. 'I am sorry. Would personal apologies help?'

'You keeping out of things will help.'

He nodded. He was going to keep out of everything from now on. He was going to go abroad and forget all about this mess and let Maggie get on with her life, despite his best attempts to sabotage it. He would make himself a better man, and everyone else would be better off without him.

'Right, on with you,' said Dr Fitzroy finally. As David turned to go, he held up his hand. 'You should think about the comprehensive sector, you know. I don't think they can afford to be picky these days. Even if we have had to let you go.'

'Thanks,' said David. But all he wanted to do was get as far away as possible and lick his wounds, and try and forget that he had caused all this trouble.

Chapter Five

Anne Adair was curious, and very, very concerned, as she went to pick her little sister Margaret up from Glasgow Central station.

Ever since Maggie had started at the posh school two years ago, much against the family's wishes – or Anne's at least – there had been an atmosphere between them, though they'd always been so close.

In Anne's opinion, there were plenty of schools here in Glasgow that were crying out for new teachers, young, energetic blood to help the kids who desperately needed it. Maggie doing all that training and going to work with posh young madams – and *English* posh young madams at that . . . well, Anne hadn't approved. But it was her life.

Except it wasn't just her life. Anne had two children, by a stupid, feckless man she knew she should have thought twice about at the time, and Cody and Dylan weren't doing anything like as well as they ought.

She tried to help them with spelling and stuff, but her spelling was terrible to begin with, plus she couldn't shut the salon till 8 p.m. and they were always busy on Saturdays; then she had cashing-up to do, and frankly, by the time she got home after being on her feet all day, she was so tired she could weep, and the last thing she could face was fighting with the boys about their homework when all they wanted to do was play on their PlayStation and eat pizza in front of the telly. She knew she ought to be doing better.

But she wasn't lucky like Maggie, who had always loved books and would read all day and who had her lodgings provided for her at this fancy school and no children and not a care in the world, and Stan, who would do literally anything for her and whom Maggie treated, in Anne's eyes, completely terribly. Now she was being all weird about getting married – a wedding Anne had never had – and Anne wanted to shake some sense into her.

She was thinking all of this, and how she should give Maggie a piece of her mind, and by the way, hadn't she noticed Mum was getting a bit wobblier and didn't she think she ought to be up more often, seeing as she didn't have any children to look after and nobody to please but herself, which included turning up a day late and putting everyone's schedule out of whack – all of this was going through her head when she saw Maggie descending from the train at Glasgow Central, her mass of red curls bright against her black coat and her face so woebegone that all thoughts of a row went out of Anne's head and all she could think about was here was her baby sister, and she was clearly miserable.

Maggie didn't want to burst into tears right in the middle of the huge station, with announcements booming overhead and people running everywhere. On the other hand, she wasn't sure she could wait, and she certainly didn't want her mum and dad to see it.

'Can we go and sit down somewhere?' she said.

They found a spare table at a coffee shop and Anne fetched them both tea rather than coffee, figuring that getting more agitated wasn't exactly what Maggie needed right at that moment.

'Tell me all about it,' she said.

Maggie closed her eyes. She had kept the way she felt about David a secret from everyone for so long, it felt ridiculous to be able to talk about it at last.

'I . . . I . . .'

She knew she sounded melodramatic.

'I fell in love with one of the other teachers.'

Anne blinked.

'I thought they were all girl teachers. *Oh!*'

'No, no. A boy teacher. At the boys' school.'

'What do you mean, fell in love? Did you have an affair?'

'No.'

'Did you sleep with him?'

'No.'

'So. It's nothing then. Oh Maggie, did you get yourself all wound up for nothing?'

Maggie felt herself flush bright red.

'No. I mean, it's serious.'

'You've both decided this? You can't have.'

Maggie bit her lip.

'I'm not sure I can get married.'

There was a very long pause.

'You don't mean that.'

'I do.'

Anne sipped her tea.

'Are you sure it's not just pre-wedding jitters? It sounds like nerves to me, Maggie.'

'It's not,' said Maggie defiantly. 'I . . . I really, really have feelings for him.'

'Is he married?'

'He was . . . engaged.'

'Oh, for crying out loud. Do you realise how ridiculous you sound right now? You're mooning about some bloke you haven't even slept with.'

Tears ran down Maggie's cheeks and one plopped into her mug.

'So. You're together now? Where is he? Is he here?'

Maggie shook her head, and started crying so hard she couldn't speak.

Anne didn't want to be unsympathetic. But Maggie had absolutely no idea what life was like in the real world.

'So, what? You're going to break Stan's heart? Ruin everyone's plans? Cancel the wedding? Spend the rest of your life alone? For some bloke you liked on Facebook.'

Maggie snivelled. 'I don't know. And he's not on Facebook.'

'Honestly,' said Anne, but not unkindly. 'Can't leave you alone for five minutes.'

She patted Maggie's arm.

'Don't rush into anything, Mags.'

Maggie shook her head.

'No,' she said. 'I'm sure.'

Anne was exasperated. Maggie had everything: *everything*. And she didn't even realise it. Whereas if Anne didn't get back in the next half-hour, Cody would be doing something appalling to their mum's cat again.

Maggie looked up.

'Can you not tell Mum and Dad for now? Until I've had the chance to talk to Stan?'

'So you've not made your mind up?'

Anne felt so sad. Stan was one of the family. He had been for a very long time; he and Maggie had been together since school.

'I think ... I think I have,' said Maggie, staring at her hands.

'You can't do that to that poor boy,' Anne hissed. 'He's been through hell without you.'

'I know,' said Maggie, her face flaming.

'And you're going to throw everything away for ... for what? For some poncey English weasel who is engaged to be married to somebody else and also isn't here? Have you taken leave of your senses?'

'Maybe,' said Maggie.

'Maggie,' said Anne. 'Stan's coming round to the house tonight when he's finished his shift.'

'I know,' said Maggie.

'He said you sounded weird.'

Maggie looked out at the lines of red trains across the concourse. She wanted to take one somewhere – anywhere – to get out of here. But she couldn't.

Maggie looked at her phone as Anne went to pay for the parking. Six missed calls from Stan. Nothing from David. Nothing at all.

At home, she went straight up to her old bedroom, having told her confused mother she was going to change.

It was still there on the back of the door. Just hanging there, rustling gently in the breeze from the open window. Her wedding dress.

She fingered the soft lace through the plastic covering. She had bought the dress in the Easter holidays, hardly caring, she remembered now, because it had seemed so unimportant. Her carelessness for other people's hearts suddenly overwhelmed her, and she threw herself on the bed, sobbing hard at how she'd wrecked everything she'd known.

She'd lost track of time – the evenings were long in Glasgow at this time of year – when a gentle knocking came at the door. Oh God, her poor mother. She hadn't asked for any of this; she'd been proud of her daughter being a teacher, whether it was in the local school or the big posh school down south; she'd just been proud of Maggie, first in her family to go to university.

She rubbed her face. Her mother deserved the truth, even if the truth sounded absolutely ridiculous to her own ears. She glanced at her phone again. Still nothing from David. Oh my God, maybe he was in prison. Maybe they were keeping him in. Maybe he'd been beaten up by the other prisoners, or worse ... She felt panicky.

The knock sounded again.

'Come in, Mum,' she said in a very low voice.

But it wasn't her mother who came through the door.

Chapter Six

Felicity Prosser was concerned.

She'd Snapchatted her best friend Alice three times, and Alice hadn't got back to her, not even after the one where Fliss had put her and her dog Ranald in the puppy-ear mode. Now she was too worried to upload it to her Instagram account in case it didn't get any likes. She sighed.

Her parents looked at her from the French windows that opened onto the terrace and the steps descending gracefully to the huge lawn.

'She's just so ... listless,' moaned Annabel Prosser, her very elegant mother. 'It can't be good for her cardio.'

'She's turning fifteen,' pointed out her father.

'Well, quite. I was preparing for my season then. And getting into every nightclub on the King's Road.'

'I rather think I prefer the moping about.'

Fliss's mother sighed. 'We really should get her head out of those screens.'

Mr Prosser reflected that Annabel herself spent hours staring at Net-a-Porter and a frankly unfathomable amount of time watching *Suits* in bed instead of doing other things in bed, but knew better than to mention it.

'I wonder what she'll get up to next year,' he said mournfully.

Meanwhile, upstairs, out of sight and out of mind, Fliss's big sister Hattie was studying furiously for her exams and eating far too many chocolate biscuits, occasionally gazing jealously at Fliss lying without a care in the sunny garden. Even Ranald didn't stick with her, Hattie thought furiously, despite the biscuits. Oh no, Felicity was always the centre of attention. Last year she'd even got a mild case of anorexia, just in case anyone took their mind off her for, like, half a second. On the surface, Hattie knew anorexia was a disgusting, hateful disease. But she couldn't help being slightly resentful of how much attention it had brought Fliss, and how delicate and ethereal her sister had looked while having it. Hattie herself looked like the kind of girl who would be formidably good at hockey, and indeed she was. Her father called her Miss Joan Hunter Dunn. She hated it when he did that.

She bent over her books again. Fliss was only going into the third form; she had nothing to do once she'd chosen a few subjects. Art, drama, English and music; of course that was what it would be, thought Hattie, frowning at her geography course notes. Well. This was going to be Hattie's year. She'd show them all. She'd get fabulous marks and then they'd have to notice her. That was how it worked, wasn't it?

Alice Trebizon-Woods rolled over onto her front. They were too far from land to get a mobile signal, and frankly she couldn't be bothered logging into the ship's Wi-Fi. She'd get one of those hot stewards – tanned young Australian and New Zealand boys in white polo shirts and neat white shorts who studiously avoided looking at her at all times – to do it for her later on.

Alice wasn't a hundred per cent sure exactly whose boat this was – friends of her diplomat father, who as usual was working constantly and had lots of business to attend to – but she leaned back lazily and took nine pictures of herself looking tanned and from her thinnest angle. That should do it. Very Millie Mackintosh. She'd put one up with the public setting on, in the hope that some of her teachers would see it and realise there was absolutely no point in her going back to school when she could be starting an international Instagram career right here, right now. Everyone knew that was where the money was.

She summoned one of the boys, who appeared immediately, cheerful and red-faced in the Greek sunshine.

'Can you get the internet thingy?' she said, waving her brand-new iPhone – her third; she kept dropping the pesky things overboard – at him.

'Sure, Miss Trebizon-Woods,' he said, and she gave him a distracted half-smile in recompense.

Fliss watched in alarm as Alice posted her gorgeous pic. The water was dripping off her thin tanned thighs, her white teeth glinting in the sunshine – she looked like a model, someone untouchable; far, far older than fourteen. And as she watched, the likes accumulated: blip, blip, blip. Who even were these people? How did she know so many? Everyone in their school, it seemed; even girls way, way older than her. And half of Downey Boys, including Will, with whom Alice was supposedly in something 'casual', even though what that could possibly mean Fliss had no idea.

On her own picture there were six likes, including their friend Simone, who didn't count, her mum, likewise, and three of the lamest girls in her orchestra. But not Alice. She sighed and liked Alice's anyway. It was the only way. Two weeks in Cornwall was not at all the same as a fortnight cruising on some billionaire's yacht, however much Alice protested it was boring. Plus it hardly felt like a holiday when her parents were watching every single mouthful of food she ate. She was mostly recovered, but it drove her nuts to know they didn't trust her. She was practically fifteen; would they ever stop treating her like a kid?

Simone Pribetich shut her laptop with a thud. It was a heavy old thing that her father had brought back from his restaurant when even they couldn't use it any more, and covered in indelible grease stains, but at least you could get a connection on it, if you didn't want it to do more than two things at once. Anyway, all she ever did was like everyone's pictures on Facebook and Instagram, doggedly, as if it were her job. She never posted anything, just liked everybody else's, and had a slight and constant superstition that if she missed one, it would be noticed and she would somehow be losing in some way.

Fliss and her dog in the garden looked so cute, and they were having so much fun; she was jealous of Fliss's big house and lovely garden and generous parents. Alice looked very bored and lonely on that big boat, but she liked it anyway, just in case somebody noticed. She and Alice were technically friends – the three of them roomed together – but she was still quite scared of the beautiful, quick-tongued, insouciant girl.

She really ought to be reading *Middlemarch* – she was enjoying it, truly she was, losing herself in the romantic world of Will Ladislaw and Dorothea – but she had a far more pressing concern at hand. School was back soon, and she had a clear and very real problem: her eyebrows. They absolutely would not do.

Simone had the high cheekbones and long eyebrows of her Armenian ancestors. Just plucking them she could handle, but everything had kind of changed – like there had been a letter gone out about it or something – and now all eyebrows had to be coloured a rather startling rust colour and made into a shape nobody had ever seen a natural eyebrow in before.

She was watching a lot of how-to YouTube videos, but they didn't seem to be helping very much; they talked quite a lot about things like sculpting that she didn't really understand how to do and expensive kits she couldn't afford to buy. She watched a video of a beautiful thin white girl who looked a bit like Fliss being very perky and making lots of suggestions that she couldn't quite get to work. She stared at her own slightly doughy complexion in the mirror – she'd shed a bit of puppy fat last year under the influence of American Zelda, but Zelda had had to go back to where her father was stationed in the US and since then she'd definitely let matters slide. She'd been emailing her supposed boyfriend, Ash, but they hadn't been able to meet up, so it hardly felt necessary.

Work didn't stop for her parents in the holidays – it never stopped at all – so Simone and her brother had been left very much to their own devices, and their own devices had turned out to be a lot of doing not very much.

Fridays and Saturdays she could work in the restaurant, which gave her pocket money but also meant she ate a lot more kofta than possibly she'd intended, while enduring regular customers who'd known her all her life pinching her cheeks and asking about her posh school and whether she'd found a boyfriend or not, then, on seeing her blushes, teasing and pinching her even more. She hadn't enjoyed it at all, and if it wasn't for the expression she knew her father would adopt were she to give it up, she would have left the stupid job behind. Although the money was handy. She'd kept it all, hadn't spent a penny. Probably she should buy one of those eyebrow kits, or even pay someone at the department store to do them for her.

She nearly laughed at herself. The thought of those highly made-up, scary girls at the make-up counters at the big department store ... the idea of ever approaching them scared her rigid. No. Best get back to her books. She stroked her unwieldy thick black brows in the mirror and sighed. Zelda would have known what to do. Simone missed her. Fliss barely had any eyebrows at all and Alice had someone else to do them so didn't know what she was talking about. It would be nice to have a real friend.

Chapter Seven

It was an awkward conversation, but on balance, it was one of the easier calls David had to make. David was apologetic; Miranda in her turn was utterly offhand, pretended she was only calling his name because she didn't understand what he was doing there and covered up entirely convincingly her shock and horror that he had moved on to her ginger Scottish friend, as she secretly referred to Maggie. To be honest, she'd always rather thought that befriending Maggie was an act of kindness. If it had been Claire, the chic French mistress, that might at least have been something to write home about.

Miranda couldn't hide her satisfaction that David had lost his job. She was right. He'd been a loser all along. She would stick with Declan, the slightly wide sales rep she'd left him for. This absolutely made it clear she'd made the right choice. Stopping a train, of all things. It was ridiculous; they were adults, not teenagers. Good. Well, he'd made her choice very easy. She had talked herself into a proper high-dudgeon state by the time she hung up the phone.

David was upset by how relieved he felt.

He toyed desperately with Maggie's number. But then he hadn't heard from her. She must be furious. Or just embarrassed by him; embarrassed by the way he'd behaved. He had to stop intruding, leave her alone to get on with her life.

He felt uncontrollably sad, Stephen Dedalus licking his face as he sat there.

Well. This would not do. And as the sun went down after a horrible couple of days, he made a decision. Getting away would be good for just about everyone.

Every single one of David's friends from his university days made more money than he did, absolutely without exception. Fortunately they were the very nicest kinds of friends, who didn't ever rub it in his face, and tried to include him in the best possible way. His old seminar partner Stella insisted he come to her villa in France immediately, where she provided him with lots of newly translated European fiction she pretended she was desperate to read and knew he couldn't afford, made everyone drink nothing but the light, cheap local rosé and then left him to it (even though as soon as her still-single thirty-something London girlfriends found out that tall, clever, kind David was coming down for the summer, apparently on his own, she suddenly found herself bowled over with people 'just passing through')

After four or five days during which he hid himself in a hammock, wearing an old fedora and buried deep in Hermann Hesse, David emerged unexpectedly one morning and started making a green salad.

Stella shared a glance with Ishmael, her husband, and wandered over.

'How ... how are you doing?'

David glanced up and blinked.

'I heard from Dr Fitzroy,' he said.

He'd been entirely surprised by the phone call. David wasn't a particularly good judge of how good a teacher he was.

'Not Margaret?'

There was a long pause.

29

'Not Maggie, no.'

Stella could have kicked herself. She'd spent the last three days carefully not mentioning the girl's name. She couldn't imagine who'd do this to David; he'd been so diffident about Miranda for so long, and Miranda was gorgeous.

'Well, what did he say?' she asked anxiously.

That had been the thing. After removing him from his job, a week later his old boss had called up offering him another one.

'He says he's got a friend in the comprehensive sector, and that they'll probably take me.'

Ishmael stepped forward. He'd done Teach First before scampering off to a safe job in the City, and was feeling nervous on David's behalf.

'A local school?'

'Mmm,' said David.

'You've never taught in the comprehensive sector ...'

'They're just boys.'

'And girls,' said Ishmael, smiling. 'They do girls and boys together at normal schools.'

'Oh yes,' said David. 'But they're just kids, aren't they?'

'Some are,' said Ishmael. 'Some are savage beasts.'

David smiled politely, as if Ishmael was joking.

'Which school?'

David told him, and Ishmael looked it up on some catchment map he found online. Then he sucked his teeth.

'What's wrong?' said David.

Stella glanced over Ishmael's shoulder, saw a newspaper piece about knife crime and winced.

'Are you sure there's nothing else you'd like to do?' said Ishmael. 'Couldn't you go and work in a bookshop or something?'

'Lion tamer at the circus?' added Stella.

David shrugged.

'I'm a teacher,' he said. 'I don't really know how to do anything else.'

'Do you know how to break up riots?' said Ishmael.

'Hush,' said Stella. 'For goodness' sake, leave the boy alone.'

David ran his hands through his hair.

'Well,' he said. 'I don't have a job or a home or a girlfriend. So this might be a start.'

'I'm sorry it didn't work out,' said Stella timidly. 'With the woman at work.'

'Ha. That sounds ... that sounds strange. A woman at work,' said David, wrinkling his nose. Maggie had been so much more.

The sun had brought a few freckles out. It suited him. He let out a great sigh and Stella immediately handed him a glass of wine. He stared at it contemplatively

'No. I was a fool, Stella. An absolute idiot. It's better this way. I just have to keep moving.'

Stella kissed him lightly on the forehead.

'Keep moving with that salad,' she said. 'I think we're feeding the five thousand tonight.'

It was true. Stella's entire college sorority was coming. She hadn't realised things in London men-wise were quite so bad.

David grimaced. He'd rather have had a quiet game of Scrabble with Ishmael, but he did his best to put a brave face on regardless as the gaggle of girls descended.

Chapter Eight

If Stan hadn't been so gentle, it wouldn't have been so awful. He just walked into the room with a cup of tea – strong, but with sugar in it, which Maggie had actually stopped taking since she moved down south – and put it down on the battered old MFI bedside table.

'So something happened,' he said. His face was pink, and he was wearing old jeans with a rip at the knee. He needed a haircut; he must, Maggie suddenly realised, have been waiting till just before the wedding to get one

He stood by the opposite wall; the bedroom was so tiny he was barely two feet away.

'Is this to do with him?'

There was no need to specify who 'him' was. Maggie nodded quietly.

'Well,' he said. 'So. That's that then.'

He could hardly get the words out. He glanced at the dress on the back of her door.

'Oh. Not meant to see that, was I?' He laughed, slightly hollowly.

'Stan . . . '

'No,' said Stan. 'No. Seriously, Maggie. I gave you so many chances . . . you know I did.'

'You're . . . ' She couldn't believe what she was about to say, even as the words were coming out of her mouth. 'You think we should . . . call it off?'

'What, just because you're in love with some other bloke? Maybe, yeah. *Christ*, Maggie.'

His face was suddenly stained with tears as he started to yell, to really tear into her: how she'd changed; how she'd got these uppity ways and now was off with some posh bloke who wouldn't understand her, wouldn't get her, wouldn't even care.

Maggie had to just sit and take it. Let him vent. Because he was quite right. He had trusted her. She had betrayed him in every way. She deserved everything she got.

A tiny voice inside her – which sounded quite a lot like Anne – nagged at her. *Apologise. Take it back. Resign. Come home. You can still save this. Beg forgiveness. This is the last chance you'll ever have. The best, the only chance.*

'We're not good enough for you,' Stan was saying viciously. 'None of us. You left Glasgow behind a long time ago.'

'That's not true!' said Maggie. 'It isn't!'

'He's English, isn't he?'

'What's that got to do with anything?'

'Speaks all nice? Gets you out of this scummy life, huh? All ponies from now on. I've seen it, remember. I've been to England. All that money. All that soft living and fricking . . . fricking strawberries and cream.' He spat the words out. 'It turned your head completely, that effete little wanker turning up with his "Ooh, look at all the books I've read! Ooh, look at me going to university and showing off like a ponce!"'

His bitterness was absolute and Maggie closed her eyes.

'I'm sorry,' she said. 'Maybe we just grew apart.'

'Of course we bloody did!' yelled Stan. 'Because you wanted to!'

*

Dr Deveral had been more than clear to Maggie. If she made one call to David, one email, one contact, she would lose her job. He had already lost his.

And anyway, he hadn't called. Hadn't contacted her. A hundred times a day she picked up her phone. A hundred times a day she threw it down again, unable to burn her bridges with Downey House; unable to face the idea of never going there again; of staying in Glasgow, with her own family bitterly upset and disappointed, in a neighbourhood where she knew everyone and everyone knew her as the awful bitch who had jilted lovely Stan; Stan who always had a smile for the old ladies and a pint for the old sods in the bar; who was kind to a fault; who'd been taken for a ride.

There was only a tiny notice in the Devon press about rail disruption, which didn't mention either of them by name – or, rather more importantly, the school – so that was a relief. Except that it did mean Maggie having to explain to everyone, over and over again, that yes, the wedding was off, and no, she wasn't seeing anyone else. It was patently obvious that nobody believed *that*. And the problem with the fact that they'd gone to school together was that everyone knew Stan from way back. It was very clear who the villain of the piece was; the person who'd got above themselves and moved down south and thought they were too good for everyone now. Weirdly, if she'd actually turned up with a new boyfriend in tow, at least that would have been something; a reason. As it was, she just looked like she'd got too big for her boots and would be sorry. She was, not to put too fine a point on it, utterly disgraced.

In the end, seeing her mother was definitely getting a little frailer, she did the best thing for everyone: she paid for a caravan over the week she should have been getting married, up in Elie.

The weather for once was good. Cody and Dylan ran about outside, rock-pooling and playing football with the other boys on the site; they cooked sausages and played cards and her mother couldn't have been happier if she'd been in a five-star hotel in an exotic beach location. They sat, just their little family, playing rummy into the night, and nobody said a word as the wedding day came and went, and Maggie went down to the beach, where the tide had gone out, and played with the engagement ring she was going to send back, and texted Stan to say she was sorry – again – and got back a message so unbelievably drunk it was almost a comfort to know that he was in as much pain as she was.

David took himself off from his friends eventually and went hiking in Andalusia, staying in tiny fincas out of range of phones and news and fuss to try and get back to himself; to try and get over something that had never even had the chance to begin. He read *As I Walked Out One Midsummer Morning* and *Homage to Catalonia* and grew brown and even thinner, and tried not to fret too much about possibly ruining the lives of more people than just him. And the date of her wedding came – he hadn't been invited, but he'd known; of course he'd known, and he assumed it was still happening – and he took a bottle of rough red Rioja and sat under a scrubby tree in the rolling hills and drank until he wasn't thinking about it any more.

Chapter Nine

There was silence in the Pribetiches' car. In fact, Simone had desperately wanted to get the train – there was a train, direct from London, with carriages set aside on it, that you were allowed to take when you were in the third form. Apparently it was completely brilliant fun, but her parents had absolutely said no. The price of the ticket wasn't included in the scholarship, which remained problematic.

But this wasn't what was causing the silence. No, the problem was that her brother, Joel, had sat the scholarship exam for Downey Boys, and failed. He had fussed and not studied enough, and huffed the entire way down, and was now sitting in a tremendous funk.

'It's rotten, that school,' he'd said more than once. 'Absolute stuck-up crap. I'm glad I'm not going.'

'Be quiet, Joel,' her mother said.

'I wouldn't go to that bumhole if you paid me.'

'Well they were going to and now they aren't, so tough luck,' said Simone.

'You two,' said their mother, exchanging a look with their dad. They had worried about Simone for so long being too studious. Now they had the opposite problem on their hands. 'What are your aims for this year, Simone?'

'Stop being the ugliest girl in the year,' said Joel slyly. Once more Simone wanted to kick him. 'You'll have to get kissed eventually, eh?'

Simone wanted to tell him about Ash, her kind-of boy-friend at Downey Boys, tiny and furious and brilliant. They'd been exchanging emails all summer, but she couldn't bear to ask her parents to arrange a meet-up, even though, unbe-knownst to her, they'd have been absolutely delighted.

No. She thought instead of what she hoped really would please them properly.

'Actually,' she said shyly, 'Miss Adair said that if I wanted, I could probably sit my GCSEs a year early. Some of them.'

Her mother's face, turning round in shock, said it all.

'*Darling!*' she said, beaming. 'Oh my goodness! We are so proud of you. That is wonderful news. Wait till I tell your aunties!'

Her father, focusing on the road, frowned.

'You're sure it won't be too much work, *babcha*?'

Simone swallowed and looked at Joel, who was kicking his legs crossly.

'No problem,' she said, vowing there and then that she'd do it, watching the huge smile spread across her father's face. He'd left a promising career of his own to bring them to the UK. She wanted to repay him in full.

Chapter Ten

Felicity couldn't help being a little nervous at the railway station, particularly as Hattie of course was immediately enfolded by a bunch of rah-rah lacrosse players, who all looked pink in the face and outdoorsy and were wearing fleeces even though it was only September and had loud voices that carried across the whole of Paddington station and made Fliss wince. She noticed the slightly leering looks of some of the men as they crossed the terminal. Why couldn't Hattie just shut up? Why did all her friends have to have stupid nicknames like Pubes?

She hovered at the entrance to the platform – the GWR livery on the train looked very smart – scanning anxiously for Alice. Alice was meant to be getting the train, but her scatty mother was never entirely on the ball about anything, and the succession of nannies who had dragged up the three beautiful, wild Trebizon-Woods sisters, of whom Alice was the youngest, could easily be outmanoeuvred on the issue.

Just as Fliss was getting antsy, she saw Alice's long black hair swinging across her bag, which, even though it was technically a plain school bag, somehow Alice contrived to make more expensive-looking than anyone else's.

The same went for the rest of her outfit; the girls had to wear uniform on the train, then were allowed to change into civvies for the first evening. What should have been just a charcoal skirt was on Alice something short and chic. The famous blue and yellow blazer was slim-cut and neat, her white shirt cute and charming, and she'd skipped the jumper. It was almost like she wasn't wearing uniform at all, and with her long gazelle legs, elegant posture and unimpressed face, she looked far older than her fourteen years. As always when she saw her, Fliss (who was blonde and thin but always felt washed out next to glorious Alice) felt happy and a bit strange at the same time. How come Alice always knew just how to dress? If her own big sisters were (a) a model and (b) an ex-socialite, now in rehab, rather than big gallumphing Hattie, presumably Fliss too would know how to do all this stuff, she told herself crossly.

'Come on!' yelled Alice, marching past. 'We'll sit in first class and pretend it was a mistake when they find us. Oh no, hang on, my dad just sent me a new credit card. My treat.'

The whistle was blowing as they scrambled on, giggling, and proceeded to take a luxurious four-seater table rather than squeezing into the pre-booked carriages with all the other girls, which annoyed the senior girls sighing into their phones and complaining vociferously about the school's social media restrictions. (In fact, Veronica had simply refused the phone companies' offer of a mast in the grounds and had the Wi-Fi on an Enigma-style changing-code basis, so she could pretend there were no restrictions for senior girls, while in practice, getting a GIF to work was more or less impossible. Hester Nbayo in the lower sixth had been so good at cracking the password, she'd been recruited into setting it, which had thrown a spanner in the works for everyone.)

Fliss and Alice gave each other the mandatory overemotional side-kisses, then checked each other out quickly.

'How was your summer?' Fliss asked as nonchalantly as she knew how. 'Oh God, I hate saying goodbye to London.'

The train had begun to slide out, into bright sunshine and grimy walls. Alice barely gave it a glance. 'London's so boring,' she said. 'Now Capri, that's the place. Nothing even gets going till one a.m.'

Fliss nodded like she absolutely agreed.

'I just can't bear going back to school.'

'Have you heard from Simone?'

'Oh yes, she's having to drive with her family.'

'*How* embarrassing,' said Alice. 'Nobody does that in third year. Christ, I wonder who'll take Zelda's place in the dorm.'

'Oh God,' said Fliss. 'I dread to think. Some neat freak.'

'A religious maniac.'

'Oh Lord,' said Felicity. 'I hate her already. Maybe she'll be great.'

'She might,' said Alice. 'If she's joining in third year. Maybe she's been expelled from, like, nine other schools. But forget about that. I have gossip. I have so much gossip. I have the best gossip you have ever heard.'

Ismé Elgar-Phipps sat by herself in a corner of the train, scowling.

Her mother had wanted to come with her but couldn't get a day off from her job, but that was fine. Ismé didn't care. She didn't want to go to this stupid school anyway. All her friends were at Park Side in Tottenham, while she was on her way to this ridiculous white-bread affair. With boaters, for crying out loud. Seriously. They had a school hat.

Well, if the other girls at Downey House thought they were better than her, they had another think coming. She hadn't wanted to take the stupid exam, but her teachers had pushed and pushed, and the look on her mother's face . . . She had been so excited, even though she was devastated to lose Ismé. There had always been just the two of them, in their little council flat. And now Ismé was leaving. Some of her mates were pregnant already; nobody she knew on the estate was going anywhere. And that was the point, her mum said, as she trudged out to clean offices. She had put her hands on the sides of Ismé's face and looked her fiercely in the eye – or almost; Ismé was already taller than her.

'This is what it was for. This is what all of this was for. I love you, my darling. You are doing this, so help me God. You are doing this.'

Ismé covered up her nerves by pasting a bolshie look on her face and folding her arms, daring anyone to come and sit next to her on the train. She would show them. She was going to hate it, but she had no choice but to get the grades. She'd keep her head down, then go straight home again. She didn't need any of these stuck-up snobs anyway. They wouldn't understand anything at all about her life; about the streets she'd grown up on. She was going to hate it.

Alice told Fliss the entire story about Maggie and David – which she'd picked up from her driver, who'd been dropping someone else off when the whole thing went down – while also exaggerating wildly, which meant that by that evening it would be all round the school that the teachers had been caught in the middle of Exeter railway station in flagrante and had then thrown themselves off a moving train.

'Oh my God!' said Fliss. Both of them were completely unable to imagine their ancient teacher having any love life at all, never mind a tragic one. 'I am going to spew, I promise. That makes me vomit. And Mr McDonald, too!'

She immediately went pink. Fliss's crush on Mr McDonald

was old news, but persistent. It didn't make her particularly unusual among the Downey House girls.

'I hate that stupid bat Miss Adair.'

This wasn't remotely true, but Alice always enjoyed a bit of teacher-slagging-off and Fliss was happy to oblige.

'Didn't think she had it in her,' said Alice in world-weary tones.

Fliss blinked. Talking of crushes . . .

'Did you see Will on holiday?'

Will was the fourth-form boy Fliss had liked but Alice had pulled the previous year. It was a bit of a sore point, but Fliss reckoned better out than in.

'Only in passing. His family were in Mykonos. Hole of a place. Ugh.' Alice took Fliss's hands. 'Fliss, I promise, it's very casual. Honestly. I don't care.'

In fact, Will had been cool – very cool – when he'd seen Alice, and Alice had been worrying about it frantically, but she wasn't going to tell Fliss that.

'No worries,' said Fliss as blithely as she was able. 'Anyway, what did he say about . . . what happened?'

Alice leaned forward, her eyes bright with gossip.

'Mr McDonald's been *fired*!' she said in a dramatic hush. 'Just him, not her!'

'Oh my God!' said Fliss. Then she thought for a second about how often she'd been refreshing her Snapchat. 'Hang on, how come you're just telling me now?'

'Because I wanted to see your face, of course,' said naughty Alice. 'You always had a soft spot for him. You faint every time he walks in the room.'

'I do not!' protested Fliss. 'He's just . . . he's nice, that's all.'

'Is there anyone you're not in love with?' said Alice, loudly enough that a retired couple who'd obviously properly paid for their first-class seats turned around and tutted. Fliss shrank into herself. Alice didn't even notice. 'You know what this means?' she said.

Fliss blinked. 'Poor Miss Adair?' she said.

'No!' said Alice, eyes shining. 'This is *brilliant* for us. She's going to be completely heartbroken and won't be able to pay us any attention at all because she'll be crying all the time! We're going to have the best year ever.'

Chapter Eleven

Dr Deveral was walking the halls of the school, as she always did on the first day of term before everyone arrived, revelling in the temporary quiet; the fresh beeswax polish; the flowers in the reception hall. The desks were neatly lined, the beds in a row. The playing fields were trimmed perfectly, with fresh white lines; the gravel spread around the front drive. Just for a moment, everything was perfect and the stage was set for the noisy, fluttering, chattering girls to appear, ready to learn and prepare for lives far, far away from this quiet corner of south-west England

She had been rather surprised when Maggie had sent her a short email confirming that she would be returning in the autumn. She had expected at any moment to find out that she and David had ran away together, or something equally ridiculous. In fact, deep down she actually thought they were rather a good match. However, that was still no excuse for a complete breakdown in discipline. She couldn't bear the school being in the paper for anything other than commendations and prizes.

She had, though, attempted to enjoy the rest of her holiday. As she opened the French windows to her own office, a beautiful room filled with curios from her travels and pictures of the school in days gone by, as well as one or two excellent artworks from extremely gifted former pupils, she mulled over the conversation she'd had on her last night with her son, Daniel – whom she had given up for adoption when she was very young and he was a baby, and who had come to find her in adult life. Having spent much of her life alone, she had found being part of a family for the first time both strange and wonderful; particularly meeting her three grandchildren, Holly, Josh and Rufus.

During the holiday, she had insisted on treating the family – including Daniel's adoptive parents and sister – to a small farmhouse rental near the beach in Brittany. It had a little swimming pool and a barbecue and on the whole they had had a wonderful time, particularly once everyone had relaxed a little about the strangeness of the set-up. Daniel's parents were warm-hearted people who had been initially suspicious of the glamorous, rather icy headmistress, but the children and the sunshine were great levellers, and Daniel and his wife Susie found themselves able to properly relax for the first time in years on holiday, with such keen and active babysitters on duty.

It had been on the last night, after a long game of Sorry (nobody would ever play Veronica more than once at Scrabble), the children happy and exhausted, lying snoring gently under thin sheets in their beds, that Daniel, after another glass of rosé, had brought it up.

'I've been thinking,' he began.

His adoptive mother shot him a look. 'Daniel ... '

Veronica envied their easy affection. It was difficult for her to relax with him; she had spent too long setting an example for generations of Downey girls, plus there was the very real terror of insulting or upsetting him in some way that would make him withdraw from her.

'No, Mum, listen. I'm just saying. Russia isn't what it was.'

His mother was Mum. Veronica was just Veronica. Of course she was.

Veronica had had a passionate affair in her youth with a Russian seaman, which had resulted in Daniel. He had had to return to his ship, had never even known about the baby, back when Russia was behind the Iron Curtain, closed and unknowable.

'I mean, it's a modern place now. I bet you could google him, hunt him down.'

Veronica blinked.

'I don't . . . I don't think that would be remotely appropriate. And life expectancy in Russia . . . it's not long. He knows absolutely nothing about you. How truly unfair to do this to him now.'

Daniel pouted a little.

'Don't I have a right to know my real dad? No offence, Dad.'

His kindly father just shook his head and prudently removed himself to check on the children. He found these kinds of conversations awkward and didn't really like being involved. As long as they were happy, that was all that mattered.

'Ah, leave it, Daniel,' said Susie.

'No,' said Veronica, leaning forward in her wooden chair at the weathered outdoor table. They had a view of the long grass; cicadas sounded in the trees. It really was lovely. 'No, you have a right to know. I have to tell you, I can't be involved, but I can give you everything I have on him for you to do this yourself.'

Daniel nodded, and there was a brief silence.

'Oh. Great. Right.'

Nobody said anything for a minute. Then Susie stood up. 'Come on, everyone, I'll make coffee.'

And that had been that. Now Veronica had added it, rather reluctantly, to a to-do list that was already overflowing.

Chapter Twelve

The train pulled into the tiny halt at the bottom of the grounds – it made a special stop on that day only – on an utterly perfect day in early September, with the world still green, the scent of gathered-in hay in the air, but a definite undercurrent of the autumn winds to come.

They disembarked just after lunch; cars arrived throughout the day, and Dr Deveral was there, ready and waiting for all of them.

She liked to smile – but not too sympathetically; it could invoke tears, which weren't always strictly necessary – but actually she was looking out for the parents more than the children, particularly the new first years. Would they be phoning the office every two days, demanding updates on their little darlings? Complaining about limited mobile phone use? Disputing marks?

Or would they turn their backs and vanish, leaving the children to sink or swim as they pleased; going skiing without them in the Easter holidays, expecting the school to manage everything for them. She thought of Alice Trebizon-Woods, the last of the three gorgeous Trebizon-Woods girls to pass through the school. Their beautiful, much-married mother barely set foot in the school grounds. As a result, the girls were tough, sophisticated – and, Veronica thought, missing something.

She'd rather have liked to split Alice up from little Felicity Prosser, who seemed to have packed more trouble into her first two years at school than most people would manage in a lifetime, but she felt Felicity's softer instincts were useful for Alice, and they formed a hardy triumvirate with Simone, the doughty scholarship girl. Oh, and they had a space in their dorm this term. Maggie had put the other scholarship girl in there, and Veronica approved. It was good to remind Alice that not everything came at the end of a credit card you never saw the bills for, and Simone would surely be kind and remember what it was like to be new.

Oh goodness, and they would all be in the charge of Miss Adair. Please let it be true that she'd got it out of her system and was ready to buckle down – she wouldn't be the first, nor the last, but the atmosphere these days was very different, and parents were much more likely to take a dim view of these things than they had been in the past. It was worse for David, but it was bad for everyone.

The French mistress, for example, had had an affair with the Latin professor at Downey Boys the previous year. She had, at least, been incredibly discreet. Only Veronica had noticed, because she noticed everything, but she had kept it under her hat and it had finished without incident. Maggie was young, relatively speaking. And Veronica could quite understand the charms of the handsome equally young English teacher who talked too much. But ridiculous dramatic gestures were absolutely not what this school was about, and she was not sorry that there had been an end put to it.

She ran her finger along the top of one of the old portraits of headmistresses past, in this case Professor Jean Anne Wrightly, 1957–1972. Not a speck of dust. Good.

*

The drive south had taken a long time. Her mother had cried when she left. All the emotion that had obviously been held tightly in check throughout the summer had suddenly come pouring out. Anne had stood to the side, tight-lipped. Maggie couldn't bear one more conversation about maybe staying in Glasgow. Her job was the only way now she could think to escape. And although she couldn't admit it to herself, even though she couldn't speak to him, couldn't fraternise … pathetic though it seemed, she somehow felt that she'd be happier if they were sharing the same air.

'Make sure … I mean, say hi to Stan if you see him,' she said quietly to Anne as she left. They ran in the same circles; they were bound to be talking, even if Anne hadn't mentioned it. Her sister merely sniffed.

'It's your life,' she said, apropos of nothing. Cody and Dylan at least waved wildly as Maggie set off.

At last she passed the brink of the hill that led to Downey House; saw the four towers winking in the sunlight, the bright blue of the sparkling sea beyond, and she couldn't help it. Something in her chest lifted, just a little.

Then she remembered that everyone she was going to see for the next eight months would know all the gossip and everything about it, and her heart sank again.

The beds were tightly made in the little four-bed dorms, waiting for brightly coloured duvets from home. They were past the boy band stage, thank goodness; Maggie wondered what it would be this year. YouTubers, she supposed. The vast refectory was set out with neat wooden benches, waiting for the traditional high tea that greeted everyone back for the new school year. The theatre was dim, the large sports complex already resounding to a solitary ball – that would be Janie James, the keen and beloved sports mistress, warming everything up.

Outside, summer still hung heavy on the green grass and the small copse of bright trees; beyond, the sea sparkled, with sailing boats dotted around. But she knew that now September was here, the weather would soon turn; the mornings grow crisp, the huge old radiators start to do their work. It was a time of year she cherished; of new beginnings, fresh jotters and chalk, and excited feet walking the corridors, trying not to hurry down the stairs. A new term.

Chapter Thirteen

Simone was already at the school by the time the train arrived, which was irritating, as her parents insisted on hanging around and Joel was absolutely in peak annoying mode. She was wearing her school uniform, so it might at least look like she'd come in on the train, but it was utterly boiling hot, and now she was worried that she was sweating and red in the face and with little pools at the bottom of her bra.

God, where were they? And couldn't her parents just leave? They didn't need to be here; they looked so out of place. Everyone else had a Porsche or some massive Range Rover that took up two parking spaces, and the mums all had flicky hair and tiny white jeans on, and their daughters looked exactly the same. Simone's mum was wearing her stupid wedding outfit from Debenhams, including the hat, because it was the fanciest thing she owned, and their car was a ten-year-old brown estate with a jewelled tissue box in the back seat.

'Look!' Joel was shouting now. 'She's totally embarrassed by you! Look at her! She wants you to go in case you show her up in front of her rich friends!'

'Shut *up*,' said Simone fiercely.

'Is that true?' said her mother. 'That's not true, is it?'

'Of course not,' said her father, who understood exactly the realities of life as it was for them. He patted his wife on the shoulder. 'You look lovely, Demetra.'

And then Simone felt ashamed, because her parents loved each other and her so much, and worked so hard for her, and there was absolutely nothing wrong with her life, technically, and this made her even more awkward.

'I just don't want you to get caught in the traffic,' she said. 'All the holidaymakers are heading back to London; it's awful for everyone.'

'But I thought we could have picnic here,' said her mother. As usual, the car was absolutely laden with food, as though for a siege. 'Is such a lovely day.'

'You're not allowed,' said Simone instinctively.

'*They* are,' said Joel, pointing out a very smart family who had a huge wicker picnic basket in the back of their car and were setting out folding tables and chairs and appeared to think they were at Glyndebourne.

Simone blinked hard.

'Well . . .'

Just then, her form teacher stopped by. If Simone had been looking carefully, she would have seen that Maggie looked thinner, smaller somehow; sadder. But to Simone, Miss Adair was just a teacher, a grown-up, and even though she was among the more sensitive of the girls, nothing could quite permeate her own feelings of being a hard-done-by teenager.

'Hello, Simone!' said Maggie as cheerfully as she could manage. Simone said hello back in the same slightly eager-to-please way she did everything, and her face didn't change, which meant, Maggie realised, that she didn't know. Well. For now. Veronica had been quite clear that it would be all over the school and had recommended ignoring it and giving

53

them nothing to feed on. Maggie hated thinking about it, so considered this good advice.

'Hello, Mr and Mrs Pribetich. Did you have a good summer?'

Maggie couldn't have known it in a million years, but Simone's parents instantly took this as a polite way of telling them to clear off, and started to repack their picnic into the car.

'Yes thank you very much goodbye,' said Mrs Pribetich. Simone knew her mother's accent always came in more strongly when she was nervous, and it drove her potty.

'Did you get away?'

Everyone froze.

'Very busy with business,' said her father. 'Bye now, Simone. You be good girl. Work hard, yes? Have fun also.'

Simone found herself caught up in an embrace between her parents, her brother smirking his way back to the car. Her mother started pushing bundles of food into her hands, then they pulled shut the clunky, slightly rusting old doors and took off, leaving Simone standing in the car park with two piles of luggage and four Tupperware boxes

'They're lovely, your mum and dad,' said Maggie, and Simone nodded sceptically and picked the bags up, feeling, even though it was her third year at Downey House, as trepidatious as ever.

Every year in Downey House you moved up a floor, the highest being the greatly admired fifth, or 'penthouses', as they were sarcastically known; after that, the sixth-formers lived semi-independently in converted cottages in the school grounds, where they were supposed to cook for themselves and not get up to more mischief than was strictly necessary.

The third floor was the first to have a full view of

the sea beyond the headlands, and Simone stood at the window. Plantagenet House was the nearest tower to the sea. According to jealous non-Plantagenet girls, this made it colder than the other towers; Plantagenet girls claimed it made it better.

They had been very lucky this year and had been granted one of the turret rooms, of which there were only four. There were two beds right by the window, with amazing views across the green headland and over to the sea – currently light blues and greens, but it could easily change in a second in the Cornish winter to deepest greys and tearing rain. Simone would have loved one of those beds. At home, her view was of the bins. If she had been Alice, of course, she would just have gone and bagged one. Even Fliss probably wouldn't have thought twice about it. Just put your stuff on it, she told herself. But she held back, still feeling she didn't want to get in the way, upset the pecking order, even though she'd known these girls now for two years. Could that ever change?

She clutched her old suitcase, which still had her grandfather's initials on it, its cardboard stuffing spilling out. Should she? Did she dare make a claim?

Suddenly the door burst open, and Fliss and Alice were jumping on her and hugging her and screaming, and she felt bad for having thought mean things about them even when they bounced straight to the window beds without a second thought.

'Oh my God oh my God it's been ages!' squealed Fliss, watching Simone take out her new year's books, already well thumbed. Oh goodness. She wasn't at all in the mood to be getting down to work, and hadn't done any of the reading. Neither had Alice, but Alice didn't give two pins. She looked at Simone properly. 'Look at your . . . ' She stopped herself.

'I know,' said Simone, flushing a dark red.

There was no denying it. Over the summer, Simone's bust had grown, and grown and grown.

'I am so jealous,' said Alice, who had tiny perky boobs that made her look chic. Simone envied them more than she had ever envied anything in her life.

She glanced down at her huge chest.

'I must have stopped now.'

'They're like *porn* boobs,' said Alice. Fliss shot her a glance. 'What? I mean, *amazing.*'

Poor Simone went even redder.

'They run in the family. My mum always said I was going to get them.'

'Well, you really have.'

'What size are you?' said Fliss. She was basically flat-chested, didn't really need a bra at all. Her mother kept telling her this was a good thing, but she didn't feel that way at all. It made her look nine, and ensured that no boys looked at her ever. Simone's were unmistakable, though, even under a big jumper.

Simone winced. 'Thirty-six double D,' she murmured. Both the girls whistled.

'That's amazing,' said Alice. 'You'll be able to have your pick of anyone.'

'I don't want my pick of anyone.'

'What about Ash? Didn't you see him over the summer?'

Simone shook her head and there was an awkward silence.

'I don't even know why men like tits so much,' mused Alice, throwing herself on the bed. 'They're just like big bags of fat.'

The other girls nodded in agreement.

'Very big, in my case,' said Simone. 'My bras are absolutely horrible.'

'You can get nice bras for big knockers,' said Alice. There was another silence as they remembered that Simone's family didn't have much spare cash, and Fliss secretly pledged to buy her something nice for Christmas.

'Hattie will be jealous,' said Fliss. 'She's always moaning.'

'She has got tits,' said Alice. 'It's just she has shoulders about a mile wide, so they're really hard to see. They're like two loaves of bread on a duvet.'

Fliss and Alice laughed nastily, and Simone smiled wanly. She'd forgotten school was quite so full on.

'Oh!' said Fliss. 'And you have to tell her about Miss Adair!'

'Ooh yes,' said Alice, rubbing her hands. 'I want to tell everyone, by the way. I'm taking charge of telling.'

'What?' said Simone. But just then there came a knock on the door.

Chapter Fourteen

Ismé stared up at the circular staircase in disbelief. She was expected to climb this stupid Hogwarts thing every day? Her bags had been taken off the train by a porter and brought separately to the school, which she disapproved of already. Everywhere girls were rushing back and forth screaming like idiots with joy at seeing each other again. She could do without that.

She turned up at her assigned form room, only to find nobody there. Maggie tumbled in five minutes late, her mind still slightly frazzled from being back at Downey; her heart still trying to ignore the emptiness that lay only a little way away in the boys' school over the hill.

'Ah, hello,' she said somewhat breathlessly, her red hair bouncing down her back. She tried to make up for her tardiness with enthusiasm. 'You're Ismé!'

She hadn't met the girl at the interviews. Ismé had originally been in line for Tudor, and in fact had only slotted into Plantagenet because Zelda had left. Veronica, interviewing the clearly incredibly intelligent but sullen girl with the chip on her shoulder, had thought that the firm, no-nonsense Miss Starling would be a better fit than Maggie, who had a disappointing occasional tendency towards chip-shouldering herself. However, the school was, thankfully, booming, and this was the only space they had.

Maggie fumbled around for the notes that had been sent over; Ismé stood with her arms folded.

'Did you have a good trip here?' she said, playing for time.

'S'all right,' said Ismé.

Maggie glanced up. Ismé was an exceptionally pretty girl: long curly hair, mid-brown skin, surprising green-flecked hazel eyes. Her expression now was fierce. Maggie's heart went out to her. She knew it wasn't easy to show up on the first day of term; she'd done it herself. Especially not in the third year. She slowed down and took a breath.

'Do you want to sit down and have a cup of tea?' she asked kindly. Ismé shrugged and slumped in a chair as Maggie went down to the kitchens. Fortunately Joan Rhys, the talented and cheery chef, was on hand, and even slipped a couple of cherry slices onto a plate. Maggie smiled in gratitude. Joan patted her arm sympathetically, which made Maggie realise suddenly in horror that the cake wasn't for Ismé; it was for her. That of course the story would even have reached the kitchens.

'Right . . . thanks,' she said.

Back in the form room, she put the tray down. 'So, originally you weren't assigned to this house and you'll have met Miss Starling. But now you're going to be with us, so do you want to tell me a little bit about yourself?'

Ismé rolled her eyes.

'Is it not on the form? You guys can read, right?'

'Excuse me?' said Maggie. In response, Ismé sat back, tutted and rolled her eyes.

Funnily enough, a couple of years ago, Maggie would have been more sympathetic to this kind of behaviour; she was used to it in the school she'd left behind. But there were high expectations of Downey girls in their behaviour and standards of courtesy, and it wouldn't be fair to Ismé to think they wouldn't apply to her.

She leaned forward.

'Ismé,' she said, 'you are very welcome here. Downey House is lucky to have you, not the other way around, and we appreciate that. However, everyone here, in every year and every position, has a responsibility to respond to other people with politeness and respect. We would like everyone in the world to respond to other people with politeness and respect. Unfortunately that doesn't happen. But in here it does. Do I make myself clear?'

Ismé paused for a second. Then she nodded slowly. Maggie could see it in every blink, every second, the girl working out how far she could go; whether she truly wanted to stay; the weight of the hopes and fears she'd brought with her.

'Don't worry,' she said, relenting and pushing over a cherry slice. 'I know it seems really strange and stuffy here. It did to me when I got here two years ago. But it's a pretty decent place really.'

Ismé looked up, refusing the cake. Maggie had already tucked into hers; Joan's cooking was fantastic.

'Are you worried about missing your mum?'

Up until then, Ismé had been holding it together, no problem. She wasn't going to be soft-soaped into anything. And she was fourteen, she wasn't a child. To be asked something so direct took her by surprise and she almost burst into tears.

'Honestly,' said Maggie quickly. 'It's perfectly normal. Is she really, really pleased you're here?'

Ismé blinked quickly. What the hell was wrong with her?

'I'm all she's got,' she said quietly.

'Well, isn't she lucky,' said Maggie. She stood up, a tad briskly. It wouldn't help to dwell. 'Come on, I'll show you

60

your room. You've hit the jackpot: new girls never, ever get turret rooms. It's absolutely your lucky day.'

She showed Ismé upstairs, briefly saying good evening to Alice and Fliss – one look at Alice's dancing eyes told her she already knew everything there was to know about her and David – then retreated as quickly as she could. She reckoned Ismé would settle in easily enough; she seemed a decent sort really.

Simone grabbed her on her way downstairs.

'Hello,' said Maggie, genuinely pleased to see the bright girl again. 'Glad to be back?'

'Yes,' said Simone, going bright red. But this could be for any reason, Maggie rationalised to herself. 'Um. I want to speak to you. About my exams. I do want to take them this year – as many as I can.'

'Oh Simone, that's wonderful news,' said Maggie. 'For ambitious girls like you, it's the best thing to get them sorted. I'm sure it won't be a problem. Well done, you.'

And Simone, despite all her worries about her breasts, and whether Ash still liked her, and what the dorm was going to be like this year, suddenly felt ten feet tall.

'You think I can do it?'

'Work hard,' said Maggie, 'and you can do anything.' And for once, she absolutely meant it.

Chapter Fifteen

Simone had totally forgotten, as she swept in cheerfully, that there was going to be a new girl, but while she'd been talking to Miss Adair, Ismé had started to unpack.

Fliss thought, oh, great, another really thin, beautiful girl, rendering me invisible yet again.

Sharp-eyed Alice, checking out the cheap luggage, the fake leather bag and shoes, thought, oh God, another scholarship girl with all their boring hang-ups and right-on politics. Why couldn't she have got someone more like her, so she wouldn't have to dial down talking about her own life all the time? After all, it was supposedly a privileged school.

Simone felt nervous meeting new people whoever they were.

'Hey,' said Alice coolly.

''Sup,' said Ismé equally coolly. Fliss glanced up. This sounded American and impressive in a way she could never pull off.

'Hello,' said Simone timidly. 'Um, would you like this bed? Mine's just here.'

'Four to a room?' said Ismé. 'Seriously?'

'We've got our own bathroom,' said Simone. 'And a view.'

Ismé sighed and looked at the tiny wardrobe.

'So where are you from?' asked Alice. 'London?'

'Yeah. Why?'

Alice blinked slowly.

'No reason.'

Fliss was going to say that she thought Ismé looked cool and street but decided against it. She did, though. She looked like she should be in a music video. Fliss wasn't sure if that was racist.

'Whereabouts in London?' said Simone hopefully. 'I'm from there too.'

'Yeah, it's scholarship central,' said Alice. They all looked at her. 'What?' she said. 'Sorry, are you not on a scholarship?'

'Is that a problem?' said Ismé.

'No, not at all,' said Alice. 'Simone is too.'

'It's really nice to meet you,' said Simone, who was absolutely delighted to have someone who would understand life on the scholarship plan – the paperwork, the pressure, the family stuff that came with it. Fliss looked over, slightly jealous.

'So, there's like apartheid here?' said Ismé.

'Yup, that's exactly what it's like,' said Alice, rolling her eyes. 'Actual apartheid. We never hang out with you at all, do we, Simone?'

Simone smiled. 'It's all right,' she said to Ismé. 'Don't worry. It's okay here.'

Ismé started unpacking her clothes.

'A lot of people keep telling me not to worry,' she mused. 'People rarely say that about things that don't need worrying about.'

Chapter Sixteen

'*Salut, ma copine!*'

'Oh Claire!' said Maggie joyfully. She was delighted to see her friend, the chic French mistress, with whom she shared a set of rooms: a small bedroom each and a comfortable sitting room and bathroom. She had sent her an email explaining everything. Unfortunately Claire had made it perfectly clear that she was uncontactable throughout the month of August, doing mysterious French things. Anyway, it wasn't the kind of subject that could really be discussed online or in a phone call. It needed a bottle of wine and some face-to-face time.

"Ow are you, *cherie*?' Claire took one look at her friend's face. 'Don't answer zat. Oh, *mon bout*. These men, these men, you know, they make us so *crazee*.'

Maggie shook her head sadly.

'I know.'

'And you 'ave seen him?'

'No,' said Maggie. 'Not at all. Veronica asked me not to contact him if I wanted to stay here. So I didn't. And he hasn't contacted me either.'

She sat down on the sofa. The entire day had been rather overwhelming, even without the long drive. She buried her face in her hands.

'And I know all the girls know and are laughing at me.'

Claire gave out a very Gallic snort.

'They are leetle eediots. Nobody care what they think. And it will be five minutes, pouf, *fini.*'

'Oh God. I don't think I can go to dinner.'

The first night back there was a large traditional dinner for the whole school. Dr Deveral would say a few words, and all the teachers had to sit on the raised platform (normally things were much more informal, and the girls ate at different times). Maggie envisaged the whispered comments and the gloating eyes on her, not to mention some jealous ones: Mr McDonald had been very popular at Downey House, where he often helped with drama productions, and there had been many deep crushes over his dark looks and ready smile. She realised that they were teenage girls and she was a grown-up and ought to be able to brush it off, but she was dreading it.

'Bah! *Oui, bien sûr,* dinner will be bad, and then it will be forgotten.'

'Do you think?'

'I already have forgotten it.'

'Have *you* ... heard from him?'

'*Non,*' said Claire sorrowfully. 'You know he has left?'

Maggie realised there had been a bit of her hoping that she'd been misinformed. Or that he'd decided to leave and then changed his mind. Now, that final piece of hope had gone.

'Right,' she said. 'Yes. Quite right.'

"Ow was home?' said Claire. Maggie just shook her head. She couldn't bear to think of it.

Claire got up and went to the fridge, returning with a bottle of rosé.

'Normally before dinner I say, pff, *non.* Today I say *oui.* One glass. And if they make bad things to you, I shall give them extra homework in the sobjonctive and the past literary *aussi.*'

She poured a glass for Maggie, who took it, grateful beyond measure for the friendship.

Veronica saw Maggie slip in, not her usual bouncy self at all. She knew this wouldn't be easy for her, and had some sympathy. She looked out at the shining faces in front of her, some sulky, some nervous, many happy, and reminded herself with a touch of steel that it wasn't about Maggie. It was about Downey House, and having the best available for the school. And Maggie was a superlative teacher, even if, at the moment, she was clearly suffering from lovesickness just as badly as Astrid Ulverton, a highly talented clarinettist who'd spent the summer at orchestra camp and had to be physically disentangled from a bassoon player. Even now she was surrounded by her thrilled friends, offering tissues and revelling in the drama. Astrid would never in a million years think she understood. She did, absolutely.

When everyone was seated, Veronica stood up, and there was instant hush. The new first-year girls were nearest the front, and she searched their faces for signs of bravado or fear. Some were away from home for the very first time. It seemed that children were independent later and later these days. In some ways it was good – there were fewer scrapes and less drinking among the older girls than there used to be. In other ways, they were so cosseted, so protected from life, Veronica worried slightly that it would damage them.

It was her job to expose them more to the world; not the real world, of course – Downey House would never be that. But to a world where you were responsible for your own work, your own timekeeping; where Mummy or your nanny wouldn't be running behind you picking up your clothes, tidying your wardrobe and making excuses for you. Life was full of knocks, however wealthy your parents or privileged your existence, and keeping children away from it so that everybody lived in a state of arrested development until they were forty – she wasn't sure that was the best way forward.

'Welcome back,' she said as the room quietened. 'I hope you have had productive and happy summers. Or happy summers at least.'

This was about as close as Veronica was capable of getting to a joke, and most people tittered politely.

'For those of you new to Downey House, you are very welcome. We hope you will love your time here and become a happy and supportive member of our community, as many generations of girls have done over the years. Our aim here is the same as it has always been: to produce women – brave, independent women – who know their own strengths, who know how to make the best of what they have. Not just in sport, or academia, although we expect your best efforts in all you attempt. We hope you learn more here. Constancy, decency and kindness . . . '

Seated halfway back, Alice gave a very small snort, and Fliss nudged her.

' . . . a feeling of being in the natural world, and respecting it and each other, so that when you leave here, you will always carry us with you, as you go wherever fate and life take you. Now, some notes . . . '

And Veronica nimbly listed the whereabouts of some recent old girls: Mhari Wansted, now an army officer serving in Iraq; Natasha Vladinishkov, doing research into Alzheimer's deep in the jungles of Venezuela. It was inspiring stuff, and Maggie felt herself calm down a little. Maybe it was going to be all right. You always got that sense with Veronica around. She was definitely one of the grown-ups.

As Veronica sat down to applause, supper was served and Maggie pulled her chair forward to eat, noticing for the first time that her boss, the disapproving head of the English department, was sitting right beside her.

Miss Starling had been at the school for years – Maggie privately thought she'd been grown in the chemistry lab. She was part of the fabric of the building; no family of her own. The school meant everything to her and she was an absolute stickler for the rules. She had always disapproved of Maggie's more laid-back approach and hadn't liked the fact that she came from a comprehensive school. Now Maggie realised that everything that had happened had just validated what Miss Starling had thought about her all along.

The older woman regarded her with her pale, clear eyes.

'Hello, Miss Starling,' said Maggie, again feeling like one of her teenagers. 'Did you have a lovely summer?'

Miss Starling sniffed. She didn't particularly like enjoying anything.

'The fjords were perfectly bracing, thank you.'

They continued eating in silence. 'So this year we're scheduled to start with the romantic poets . . . ' ventured Maggie.

Miss Starling turned that pale gaze on her.

'Shouldn't be too much trouble for you, then.'

'Excuse me?' said Maggie. She felt her face getting hot. Anger was one of her worst faults, one she was always trying to conquer, though she didn't necessarily make a great success of it.

'We've all heard about your romantic exploits. You've cost Downey Boys an excellent teacher.'

'It wasn't me! It wasn't my idea! None of it was!' said Maggie, horrified by the injustice.

'Well, there's no smoke without fire, so they say. Everyone saw you flirting and messing around. I can't believe you're back here, frankly. If I were headmistress . . . '

Maggie's cheeks blazed, and although it was absolutely the

worst thing under the circumstances, she found she couldn't stay in case she said something she regretted.

'Excuse me,' she said through gritted teeth, pushing back her chair. Unfortunately it squeaked horribly on the ancient wooden floor, and the entire room looked up.

Veronica glanced over, concerned. Oh goodness, please say June Starling wasn't being moralistic again. She should have known better than to let them sit together; it was an unforgivable oversight.

Maggie was doing her best to hold it together, even though she knew her bright red face was giving her away and that girls everywhere were pointing and nudging each other. As she walked past the third-form table, Fliss wanted to reach out to her to see if she was all right. Alice sighed and said, loudly enough for Maggie to hear, 'Oh, heartbreak is *such* a terrible thing,' and it was all Maggie could do to collapse out into the corridor before the tears started to fall.

Chapter Seventeen

Maggie hadn't sobbed on her bed for long – comforted by Claire, who didn't actually eat the meals at Downey House, finding them entirely too stodgy for her tastes – when the internal phone rang and she was summoned down to Veronica's office.

It was growing dark outside, the long evenings of summer beginning their retreat, but it was a clear night and you could just see from the west window the sun setting over the purple sea.

'Are you all right?' enquired the headmistress almost at once.

'I shouldn't have come back,' said Maggie. 'I think maybe ... after the scandal ... perhaps I should have stayed in Scotland.'

Veronica glanced up briefly from some paperwork she was looking at.

'Nonsense,' she said. 'How would that look? As if Downey girls simply run away from the merest difficulty.'

'Well, I wouldn't care,' said Maggie ungraciously. 'Because I'm not a Downey girl, and because I'd be in Glasgow.'

'Would you?' said Veronica quietly.

Maggie thought back to the awkward atmosphere, the strange situation and, more pertinently, the fact that the person she'd shared half her life with wasn't actually talking to her. Things weren't any better there. She shrugged.

'Now, you know Miss Starling is old-fashioned. She says she didn't directly mention anything. Is it at all possible you're being oversensitive?'

Maggie's face was a dull red. She knew this was probably true. Any allusion to any mention of David was like a needle in her flesh. There was a long silence.

'It's possible,' she said eventually, toying with a tissue on her lap.

'It is,' said Veronica. 'If you had simply smiled and said, "Oh, all that is behind me," do you see how it might have defused the situation?'

'But ... ' said Maggie. And then, 'Yes. Okay.'

'And don't you think that if you walk into your classes tomorrow with a smile – even though you have now, of course, dialled the rumour mill up a hundred per cent with your little flounce ... '

Maggie squeezed her eyes shut. Oh God. Of course she had. In front of the entire school.

' ... don't you think everything will blow over?'

'Yes.'

'Yes. It will. Now, you have a lot – and I mean a *lot* – of work to do. I hope you finished your lesson plans over the summer, rather than just mooning about.'

'Oh yes.' In fact, Maggie had worked harder than ever simply because she didn't have anything better to do.

'Good. Then go and do your job, please. No more tantrums.'

Maggie nodded and turned towards the door, chastened. As she touched the old metal handle, Veronica spoke again.

'Don't think ... do not think I'm not sympathetic,' she said.

Maggie nodded mutely and darted off.

Chapter Eighteen

Back in the dorm, Simone was finally learning the whole story, or rather the whole story as filtered through Alice.

'She did *what*?'

'She led Mr McDonald on! She stopped a train for him!'

Ismé, who had already got ready for bed, was pretending not to listen but was actually taking it all in.

'But she had a boyfriend! That weird Scottish guy who came down to watch the hockey.'

'I know,' said Alice salaciously. 'Looks like she was doing the dirty with Mr McDonald all the time.'

'He *is* very attractive,' said Fliss dreamily.

'He's an old man,' said Alice. 'He must be at least thirty.'

'He's thirty-four,' said Fliss. Then, as everyone stared at her, 'What? So I googled him, so what. He's won awards and stuff.'

'Well, I think it's disgusting,' said Alice. 'No wonder she's such a mess.'

Simone thought about it.

'It's weird to think about grown-ups getting into relationships and stuff. Like your parents doing it. Yuck!'

'Not for me,' said Alice, whose mother looked like she was getting married for the fourth time.

'I think it's romantic,' said Fliss.

'You think everything's romantic,' said Alice. 'You'd snog the gardener.'

'I would not!' said Fliss. 'Hang on, there isn't a new one, is there?'

In truth, Fliss felt like the world's most under-kissed girl – at fourteen, she hadn't even had her first kiss, whereas Alice and even Simone had both managed to pull boys in the second year. The closest she'd ever got to a male she wasn't related to was when Mr McDonald had had to pick her up after she'd fainted. It wasn't her fault she'd got slightly infatuated.

'Well, I just hope she doesn't drip tears all over the set texts,' said Alice, glancing at her new timetable and sighing. 'Why the hell is English compulsory? I don't have to take bloody German any more.'

'You're good at German,' said Simone loyally. It was true. Alice spoke a smattering of lots of languages, picked up from being dragged around the Continent as a child.

'Swiss German,' said Alice dismissively.

Fliss glanced over at Ismé, who was pretending to read her Reni Eddo-Lodge book.

'You must think we're all crazy,' she said.

Ismé looked at her levelly.

'At my last school, someone got knifed on the first day,' she said. 'So no, not really. It's all very ... ' She flapped her hand and sighed. 'A bit schoolgirl, you know what I mean?'

The other girls exchanged glances.

'Well, maybe that's because—' started Fliss.

'Oh, leave it,' said Alice, as the prefects on the corridor shouted, 'Lights out!'

Chapter Nineteen

The streets leading to the school were a filthy mess. Bins were presumably emptied, but even so there were overspilling bags of litter everywhere. Plastic bags bounced in the wind; it was an unusually chilly day, and David turned up the collar of his old overcoat.

There was a metal detector on the gates of Phillip Dean Comprehensive Secondary School, and a buzz gate, even though the students were currently on holiday.

The place was vast: nearly three thousand students. Very few of them went on to university; forty per cent left with no qualifications at all. David ran through the stats in his head. Eighty per cent on free school meals; sixty-five per cent had English as a second language, although why speaking two languages was seen as a drawback he had absolutely no idea. There was a constant police presence in term time, and it was the single least popular school in Darne, one of Devon's largest towns. Basically, if you or your parents either didn't understand the system or really didn't care where you went, you ended up at Phillip Dean.

'It's more of a holding pen than a school really,' said the nervous headmaster, a Mr Barry Frise. He was, David found out, the fourth head in two years. 'Staff turnover is quite . . .

well. It's something,' he said before David had even taken his coat off. 'You need to be quite a sturdy character to take the job on.'

He glanced at David.

'Do you have much experience of disciplinary issues?' he said.

'Such as?' said David.

'Well, it's violence mostly. A lot of shouting. Basic insubordination. Refusing to do what they're asked. That kind of thing. Animals, most of them.' He smiled, then winced.

'They're just children,' said David.

'Half of them are about eight feet tall,' said Mr Frise. He really didn't look well, considering he could only be about David's age.

'Well,' said David. 'You need an English teacher and you've got my CV and you know I'm qualified, so it's up to you mostly. I'm happy to talk about why I left my old job.'

'Oh no, I heard . . . Teachers talk, you know,' said Mr Frise quickly, and David grimaced. 'No, that's . . . I mean, we're not quite so . . . Well. Anyway. That won't disqualify you from here. We don't have rules like that.'

David raised an eyebrow, but he was too far from his normal ebullient self to make a cheerful remark at the moment.

'If you'd like the job, it's yours,' said Mr Frise.

Surprised – he'd brought along several lesson plans and ideas for outings, as well as swotting up on some fairly depressing government guidelines about working in the public sector – David shook hands with his new boss, who gave off a faint scent of old coffee left too long and disappointment, and headed back into the small, empty concrete playground.

There wasn't a tree to be seen; all the playing fields had

been sold off and turned into executive apartments, which the children apparently regularly broke into.

It was a challenge, he tried to tell himself. Something new. But his heart felt so, so sad.

Chapter Twenty

'So this is our first lesson,' said Maggie. She had got up early and considered going for a walk – it was a beautiful autumn day – but eventually decided against it. She used to regularly run into David and his dog, Stephen Dedalus, on those walks, and she wasn't quite ready to be reminded of it.

Instead she took the opportunity to wash and style her hair carefully, press a suit and put on a full face of make-up. It made her feel better armed against the world. Claire smiled appreciatively as she made them both the thick black coffee she preferred.

'*Voilà*, all will be well,' she said. 'Please do not worry. Do not let them get to you, *petits monstres.*'

Maggie nodded and picked up her Wordsworth *Companion to English Literature*.

'I'm well armed.'

'*En fait* you need Baudelaire,' said Claire, but Maggie was already gone.

It was undeniably comforting to be back in her old classroom. It was a long room on the ground floor of the main building, with windows facing south across the playing fields and on towards the sea; it was a heavenly view. The desks were old, with flip-up lids and inkwells, generations of initials carved in the wood, but she had a modern computer board that could email the girls instantly with homework and notes. Otherwise, very little had changed over the decades. Veronica considered a grounding in the classics essential for recognising both beauty and argument, and modern styles of teaching hadn't influenced her in the slightest.

Maggie looked down at the first poem she had chosen. It had not been ideal, she reflected in retrospect, to choose their first poetry module when in the depths of heartbreak. Plus, the Pablo Neruda was going to make them snigger, but that couldn't be helped. They were fourteen. Everything made them either snigger or completely indignant. She smiled a hello as the girls filed in.

'So! This term we're going to make a start on the romantic poets.'

Instantly the class went silent, waiting for the remark. Maggie smiled as if completely oblivious.

'Wordsworth, Byron, Keats and Shelley all brought a breath of fresh air to the organised world of the metaphysical poets who preceded them – Donne, Pope, Shakespeare, of course.'

Privately Maggie thought John Donne could knock all the romantic poets into a cocked hat, but she wasn't going to mention it to the class.

'Now, who has done the reading ... Simone, yes, I see you.'

The new girl, Ismé, had her hand up too. Maggie beamed. Oh, how she loved a scholarship girl.

'Ismé?'

'Can I ask, is it all going to be dead white males?'

'Does this mean you did do the reading or you didn't?'

'Just asking.'

Maggie took a deep breath.

'I hope you'll explore the rights and wrongs of male-centred culture in your history lessons. But it's undeniable that both the men of the time and the women who came later – whom we certainly will be studying, make no mistake – built on the same body of work handed down through the years. Do I think we lost much great genius by not encouraging the talents of women back then? Yes. But the women we do have and the women who will be forging the way in the future – our new Margaret Atwoods, our new Anne Brontës, our new Maya Angelous – all come from the same tradition, hideously white as it is. These writings, and all the way back to the Bible and ancient texts, may be hideously male, as you say. But they are all we have and all *they* had, and if we are to understand our great female writers – and soon we'll be starting on *Middlemarch*, which, I promise, the less you think you're going to enjoy it, the more you will – we need to understand what they read, and the backbone of their traditions too. So. Let's make a start with Alfred, Lord Tennyson, poet laureate.'

She brought up the famous slide of his photograph, his hair a scruffy halo around his head.

'*Quelle surprise,*' said Ismé.

Maggie gave her a look.

'That's enough for now, please. Simone, could you start reading "The Lady of Shalott"?'

> '*On either side the river lie*
> *Long fields of barley and of rye*
> *That clothe the wold and meet the sky;*
> *And thro' the field the road runs by*
> *To many-tower'd Camelot;*'

read Simone breathlessly. She loved this poem, dreamed of being the doomed lady.

'The yellow-leaved waterlily
The green-sheathed daffodilly
Tremble in the water chilly
Round about Shalott.'

Maggie held up her hand. 'Thanks, Simone! Now, what do you notice from the very first stanza? What is this poet really interested in?'

Alice, unusually, put up her hand straight away. Maggie glanced at her. 'Alice?'

'Is it doomed love, miss? Is it a love affair gone wrong?'

Maggie had known it was coming. She might as well let Alice have her fun. She had always had the measure of the pretty, pert, spoiled girl, and Alice hadn't liked it one little bit. In fact, though, Maggie was harder on her than she should have been. To the outside world it looked like Alice Trebizon-Woods, with her limitless holidays and money, her good looks and effortless confidence, had it easy. Nobody could see how much time the child spent rattling around huge empty houses, checking her phone, like Eloise at the Plaza, to see which country her own mother was in. Maggie had only ever seen the privilege, not the pain.

But at that moment, the pain was all hers. She remembered Veronica's words, and Claire's.

'Actually, Alice, I was thinking quite the opposite. When there is a terrible tragedy and a love story gone wrong, Tennyson starts by talking about nothing but the foliage in the water. Does anyone else find this strange? Simone, would you like to carry on?'

'Willows whiten, aspens quiver,
Little breezes dusk and shiver
Thro' the wave that runs for ever

By the island in the river
Flowing down to Camelot.
Four gray walls and four gray towers
Overlook a space of flowers,
And the silent isle imbowers
The Lady of Shalott.'

And Maggie led them through a faintly stultifying discussion on the use of herbs and plants and nature as imagery for young girls – they became slightly more animated once they got on to orchids, and how flowers unfurled – and was pleased and surprised at the end of the lesson to find that she had got through it.

Chapter Twenty-one

Maggie was feeling tentatively optimistic as Claire collapsed on the sofa that evening, thoroughly dispirited.

'Ah *bon*, 'ere we go. 'Ow, I ask you, 'ow is it possible that so many children, they tell me, ah *oui*, my mother or my uncle or my friends, they have a *maison*, they have a *chateau* in France – in Provence, in Burgundy, yes, in Lot-et-Garonne – and *pas un mot*! Not a word of French! They cannot even ask for a baguette in the bakery!'

'It's hard to remember if baguette is a boy or a girl, though.' Maggie tried to mollify her. She had heard Claire on this subject before.

'So they spend all of August in my beautiful France, they eat her food and they drink her wine, and they do not once think to themselves, perhaps a reflexive verb might be a good thing to know, huh?'

'They're on holiday, Claire.'

'They are children! Their life is holiday!'

Maggie smiled.

'Oh, they're not too bad.'

'I hope we have nice exchange students. Last year one girl cried every day because of toast.'

'I think she was just homesick,' said Maggie. 'It wasn't just the toast.'

'Still, I do not understand—'

Maggie knew better than to let Claire go off on one of her toast rants again.

'So anyway, my day wasn't that bad.'

'Bah, *non*?' said Claire. 'That is good!'

And she knew she shouldn't, she knew she had promised herself that she wouldn't, ever. But leaning over to pour more tea, Maggie suddenly had a flash – an image of her and David sitting together, going over their day, her making him laugh with what Alice had got up to, reading 'The Lady of Shalott' to one another . . .

'Maggie! You 'ave spilled the tea! Also I do not want more tea, you strange British person! Eet ees deesgusting.'

'Sorry, sorry,' said Maggie, jumping up. 'I'll mop that up.'

And she cursed herself for being weak, and went early to bed.

Chapter Twenty-two

It was awkward, Simone thought, waking up with a new person in the dorm. She'd been with Alice and Fliss for so long, and Zelda had been such a noisy force of nature, she'd just fitted in straight away. Ismé, though, was something else. She was incredibly pretty, combing down her hair with coconut oil; she read feminist tracts that Simone hadn't even heard of, and was on her social media every single second it was allowed. Simone tried to follow her on Instagram, but her account was private and Simone was too nervous to ask in case the answer was no.

'Oh my God,' said Ismé, the second she awoke. 'Can you really not get online in the morning?'

'Seven till nine thirty p.m.,' said Simone promptly. 'And sixth-formers who live in the grounds get it all the time.'

'That's ... I mean, that's against my human rights,' said Ismé. 'I mean, I have to curate stuff.'

'Can I follow you on Instagram?' said Simone hopefully.

Ismé screwed up her face.

'Well, it's really ... I mean, it's quite a woke site,' she said. 'I'm not sure it's for you.'

'What do you mean, woke?' said Alice, rolling over. 'It's barely gone seven. The bell hasn't rung yet.'

Ismé smirked.

'Yeah, well, that's pretty much exactly what I mean when I say it's probably not for you.' And she sat up in bed and crossed her legs. 'Would everyone mind not talking for five minutes while I meditate?'

It was to nobody's credit that they couldn't, in fact, stay quiet for five minutes while Ismé meditated (or pretended to, Alice said later), but instead had to stifle their giggles under the duvet. To make matters worse, halfway through, the bell really did go, and the building erupted with one hundred girls furious to find they were back at school and the first week of term, and it was time to get to the showers and get moving. Radios were played, tights searched for, and Ismé sat still as a stone, eyes tight shut, refusing to take the joke, until the five minutes were up, whereupon she walked with dignity into the en suite and the other girls exploded in hysterics.

'This is going to be a long year,' predicted Alice.

Fliss felt sorry for her new room-mate, and a bit bad. It wasn't her fault people sneered at things here. Actually, Fliss had thought Ismé meditating had looked quite cool.

She hung back at breakfast as everyone else was greeting the friends they hadn't had a chance to see the evening before, and slipped in next to her. Ismé had grapefruit and a bowl of plain porridge.

'Sorry about this morning,' Fliss said. 'I just don't think we were expecting it.'

Ismé looked up at her with those beautiful long greeny-hazel eyes of hers and blinked slowly.

'Oh, I certainly was,' she said lazily. Then she turned back to reading Roxane Gay. 'And can I get some privacy when I'm FaceTiming my gf? Thanks.'

Fliss was dumbstruck both by the girl's casual confidence and rudeness and by the revelation that she had a girl-friend. Awesome!

Chapter Twenty-three

David arrived bright and early for his first day at Phillip Dean. He'd actually turned up the day before, just to have a good scrub-out of the drawers. The equipment was woeful and there wasn't even a school library. They were expected to download frankly dodgily provenanced texts and read them off their iPads or computers – or in some cases, where there weren't either of those things at home, their phones.

'They do their reading on their *phones*?' he'd said to Mrs Capstani, head of English, an exhausted-looking divorcee in her mid-forties who'd perked right up when she'd seen him.

'Oh yes,' she said. 'It's handier, see?'

'But don't we encourage ... quiet time for reading, away from the distraction of screens?'

He thought further and ran his hands through his hair.

'Does this mean they have to bring their phones to class?'

Mrs Capstani blinked.

'What do you mean?'

'Well, how do you get them to put their phones away?'

She laughed. 'They never put their phones away.'

'But ... how can they learn if they've got them out all the time? I know adults that can't leave those things alone, never mind kids.'

'Breaching their human rights, isn't it?' said Mrs Capstani. 'Try taking them off 'em! Ha! Good luck with that, chicken.'

'Well, they're going to be banned in my classroom.'

'Or what? You're going to exclude them? Barry will be very unhappy with you.'

It struck David that Barry Frise didn't look like a man who could be much unhappier than he already was, but he didn't mention it.

The classroom was grubby: window frames, years out of date, had gone uncleaned; chewing gum seemed to cover the underside of every desk in the room. David did the best he could to clean up, but the rows of utilitarian grey desks – so many of them: forty? – filled him with foreboding. He couldn't help it: as he scrubbed, he lapsed into exactly the kind of thing he had promised himself he wouldn't do – dreaming about what Maggie would say. How she would have teased him about it, then probably come and helped, or at the very least been sympathetic, and laughed that merry laugh of hers ...

He opened his eyes again. Outside it had started to rain, and the litter in the playground was being blown up by the wind and whirled about. The first of the pupils had started to wander in, scruffily dressed, their walks stooped. They shouted and swore loud enough to be heard inside the building. The boys, huge, many of them, bounced off one another, cuffing and playing around in a way that would have been immediately stopped at Downey Boys.

David glanced down. His fingernails were filthy. It was cold. He rinsed out his dirty cloth and carried on.

At 8.50 a.m., the first bell rang, and he washed his hands as quickly as he could and headed towards the massive barn of an assembly hall. The noise levels were absolutely riotous as pupils greeted one another after the break, screaming and shouting across the room. One couple was openly snogging. Many were on their phones. It was chaos.

Mr Frise was standing by the side of the stage, looking defeated before he'd even started, as if he was simply waiting for them to calm down. The other teachers were gossiping away to each other as if the pupils weren't there either. David didn't understand it. A second bell went, and that too was complete ignored by everybody. Finally, Mr Frise shuffled reluctantly to the front of the stage. There wasn't a microphone, and David wondered how he was going to make himself heard.

'Right, right, settle down,' he murmured, almost apologetically. Nobody took the slightest bit of notice. From somewhere at the back, a shoe sailed through the air, to loud, aggressive guffaws. Some of the bigger boys, David thought, had absolutely no business being in school at all; they were men, and if they weren't inclined to be there, everyone was in for a hell of a time.

'Settle down,' said Mr Frise again. 'It's your own time you're wasting.'

There was some laughter at the hoary old cliché. David looked at the front row of Year 7s. They looked absolutely terrified. Some defiant, some sulky, but most of them scared. This was the big school they'd heard about, and now they were here, and they were worried bad things were going to happen. David too thought that bad things were going to happen. He straightened up – the rest of the teachers were slouching, many still chatting – and faced the front.

'Well, have a good year,' Mr Frise said. 'You've all got your timetables via email.'

'I didn't get mine!' shouted a voice from the back, and suddenly a cacophony of voices joined in.

'New IT system,' said Mr Frise. 'It doesn't ... well. I'll have a look ... '

In the chaos, the school administrator slipped out, looking puce, to attempt to photocopy three thousand new timetables. Mr Frise dismissed the school into the playground, to cheering, for once, then turned around, white-faced.

'Oh God,' he said. 'Well. Here we go again.'

Finally, at about quarter past ten, the timetable cock-up had begun to sort itself out, and David's first class slouched into the room. It was a low tier of Year 10s. Mrs Capstani had obviously decided to throw him in at the deep end. They were technically being entered for their GCSEs, but if the past year's results were anything to go by, they weren't expected to get anywhere.

'Hello, hello. I'm Mr McDonald. Hello. Come in,' he said cheerily as they filed in. 'Okay, I've arranged for you to sit in alphabetical order.'

'We don't sit in order,' said one big, sullen-looking lad. 'We sit where we like.'

David smiled politely.

'Not in my class,' he said. 'Sorry. We're doing things slightly differently here.'

'Neh,' said the lad, sitting down at the back.

'Ah,' said David.

He knew one thing. Whether the boys were rich or poor, clever or less educated, you had no choice when it came to young men. There had to be a pecking order, and you had to be the top dog at the end of it. Otherwise, you were finished.

'Okay,' he said. 'Out with you. Rest of you can carry on ... Where's Ailey?'

A large girl with frizzy hair and a scared-looking expression made a small noise and slipped into the seat indicated.

'You're sending me out?' said the big lad.

David looked him straight in the eye.

'I'm offering you a choice,' he said. 'In or out.'

'You can't make me.'

David had rarely wished more fervently to have Maggie on hand. She was used to tough classes; she'd done all this in Glasgow. He remembered the morning walks they used to take on the moors, fresh and blowy, with Stephen Dedalus, and Maggie saying, 'Show no fear.' He remembered that himself from his first days in teaching. There were no second chances. You had to make sure you got it right straight away.

'Also,' he heard her saying, 'remember that being in school is better for many of them than being at home. Home is frightening, disorganised, unpredictable. Schools that don't have strict rules and boundaries turn into exactly the same sort of places, and that's cruel. It's a punishment in itself. They need you to be strict. Nobody else in their world gives two shits sometimes.'

'I'm afraid I can,' said David now. 'So. Off you pop. See you on Thursday, and I'll have a place for you. Andreas! You're here.'

An easy-going Greek-looking boy raised a hand and slipped into his seat.

The big kid, who had a beefy face, a shining nose and the heft of a rugby player, scowled.

'You can't do that,' he said.

'I can,' said David. 'I'd like to have you in my class. But it's up to you.'

There was a long moment of silence. Then the boy, whose name was Kai, sat down in the desk David pointed out, and everyone else shuffled into place. Obviously they took their cue from him.

'Right, next,' said David, not betraying his relief. He pulled out a large grey storage box he'd cleaned out earlier. 'Phones.'

Now there was an immediate clamour.

'You can't take our fricking phones!'

'I need to be on call for emergencies.'

'You're not getting your hands on mine!'

David stared down the hubbub.

'I'm sorry,' he said. 'I'm here to teach you. Can't do it with your phones on. Medically proven. In they go. If it was up to me, I'd take them away for the whole day. But it isn't. In my classroom, though, this is how it's going to be.'

'Well, screw this,' said Kai, jumping up from his chair, which was far too small for his large buttocks. 'We're keeping them! We're keeping them!'

The rest of the class took up the chant.

'We're keeping them! We're keeping them!'

'You're not stealing my sodding phone!' a tiny girl was screaming in David's face. He wasn't used to girls.

'Fine,' he said, his features stone. 'Off to the headmaster with you all. You're excluded from my class.'

And the entire room filed out, shouting, yelling and cheering as if they'd won a substantial victory, leaving David standing alone.

Chapter Twenty-four

Janie James got everyone out and moving first thing the following day. They were playing lacrosse that term while the weather was still fine and the fields hadn't yet turned into the wallowing quagmire that heralded winter and the dreaded cross-country running. Veronica had a deeply held belief that team sports were particularly good for teenage girls; gave them something to focus on other than themselves. She didn't blame teenagers for being self-obsessed; it was almost the definition of the process. But she didn't want to give them more time to be self-obsessed than was strictly necessary.

Maggie watched them from the windows of the library, where she was taking out some additional reading for the year. She glanced down the list: Mary Shelley's *Frankenstein*; *A Place of Greater Safety*; *Mad, Bad and Dangerous to Know*. If her girls didn't come out of the third form absolutely obsessed with doomed romance, she'd be very disappointed in herself.

They looked so carefree out there, shouting and tearing around the pitch, so lithe and young and free; not showing off in front of boys or being self-conscious, just jumping around like the girls they were. Except for one: she noticed the new girl, Ismé, slouching around the side of the court. She obviously didn't know what to do, which was fine; Janie was showing her. But her body language was still belligerent, and she barely tried even lifting her hand the way she'd been told. Maggie watched her, intrigued. Most of the scholarship girls were grateful; nervous, but anxious to show what they could do. She'd never met one under sufferance before. She would be sure to keep an eye.

She looked beyond the playing fields to the downs beyond, entrancingly inviting on this golden autumnal morning, the leaves just starting to turn. It would be a perfect day for a walk and ...

No, no, no. She turned away. There was plenty to do this term: getting ready for the French exchange, mountains of work and reading; and the Christmas show would be on them before they knew it. Plus she'd get on top of her admin, which had never been her strong point. She'd show Miss Bloody Starling; she'd show everyone. Downey House was all she had left, and she was going to do it proud.

The ancient library had books stacked over two levels in the old hall, so that if you were standing at the window, facing the wrought-iron staircase, it looked like they went on upwards for ever and you couldn't see the roof. Maggie looked at all the books and resolved to be the best teacher she could be. If she could be good at something, she could be good at this.

'Goal!' came an excited voice from outside, drifting across the lawns.

CHRISTMAS

Chapter One

Doing your duty, Maggie found, was fine as long as you kept busy. Very, very busy. She was up with the first bell at 7 a.m., marking or reviewing lesson plans; she even tidied up her filing system, which surprised Miss Starling no end, having become inured to the fact that Maggie was a hopeless case.

She could manage – she was too tired to cry – as long as she was busy. So she threw herself into the world of the school, volunteering for everything, looking to distract herself. And as luck would have it, the next distraction was a very big one indeed: the Christmas show.

Mrs Offili, the music teacher, was delighted to have her on board and sure they'd soon have everyone shipshape. The fourth form had written their own pantomime – Maggie dreaded to think – and the first and second forms would provide the choir and orchestra for the singing parts; could she devise something for the third years to do?

She had said yes without even thinking about it. And it was actually rather fun. She had gathered them together after prep to have a discussion about it, anticipating a certain amount of scorn, but in fact, they were far keener than she'd expected.

Fliss had form with Christmas concerts, and had been prepared to take a back seat, but Ismé had looked, for once, almost cheerful at the prospect. She hadn't backed down from her full-on stance in class at all, not a whit, even though some of the teachers had taken a rather dimmer view than Maggie and she'd had plenty of detentions, which she shrugged off. Maggie secretly admired her. She wouldn't be silenced. But as Mrs Offili pointed out, when Ismé held up a forty-five-minute class for fifteen minutes arguing that Bach should have been a woman, it wasn't really helping anyone.

Thank goodness for Simone, though, Maggie found herself thinking. With the extra workload for her GCSEs, the girl was doing very little but study.

In fact, so embarrassed was Simone by the shape of her body, and still so upset that Ash hadn't contacted her, she'd thrown herself into work and was in the library the entire time, even after Ash had tentatively emailed her. Simone had looked at the email, then, unable to decide what to do, deleted it immediately.

The year group decided upon an adaptation of *The Snow Queen*, which hadn't been performed in the school for years, and Maggie was happy to furnish them both with the play parts and copies of the original story.

To her total lack of surprise, Alice immediately flicked through to the Snow Queen part. The girl was a decent if rather mannered actress who had definite leanings in that direction. And in fact, her occasionally high-handed manner would suit the character. It was rather harder to see Simone, who genuinely could act, fitting into the role.

Maggie decided to hold auditions on a Sunday morning, before girls started getting picked up by parents, who often visited to take them out for the day

Saturdays were overwhelmingly concerned with sporting issues, but Sundays were theoretically a day off, and Maggie found them difficult. The rest of the week she was incredibly busy, and on Saturday night she and Claire could at least hunker down with a bottle of wine and some cheese Claire got illegally sent in, and watch television (which Maggie was allowed to choose).

But on Sundays, despite being surrounded by hundreds of people; despite the fact that they got a cooked breakfast, Maggie found herself unbearably lonely. She thought of what her sister would be up to with the boys; her mum and dad putting on their best and going to Mass, mostly so her mother could have a blether with all the other ladies afterwards; then a roast at home for everyone. She wondered if Stan still went there for his Sunday dinner. Probably, she thought gloomily.

She phoned every week at 4 p.m. – if she called at any other time, her mother started to panic – and they'd trade news. But light news. What her mother's neighbours had done. What was going on in the lives of people Maggie only dimly remembered from school. For the most part they seemed to all be happily getting married and popping out sprogs at a rate of knots, and it was absolutely nothing Maggie wanted to hear; it felt rather like 'here's what you would have won' when she was six hundred miles away, totally alone.

She knew her mother wasn't doing it to be mean; she didn't have a cruel bone in her body. But she also knew her mother's disappointment was real; having to explain to all her friends at church that the wedding was off had been incredibly humiliating, not to mention Father McSorley; having to face Stan's parents, who had always been very kind to her. It was a weekly penance, a reminder to Maggie that she had upended not just her own life, not just Stan's, but practically everyone she'd ever been in contact with.

It was a very, very lonely place to be.

That Sunday morning in November was bonny and frosty, white across the playing fields but without a breath of wind, so you didn't really realise you were cold until it was too late.

In the drama lab, though, behind the turreted main house, the clanking old radiators were doing their duty, hissing occasionally, rubbed bare of paint by generations of girls lounging against them to soothe chilblains and warm toes.

Maggie took her coffee cup down there, pulling on a big soft jumper that, she realised belatedly, had been Stan's. Or rather, she'd bought it for him one Christmas, and he'd discarded it in favour of his beloved football top. Glasgow boys didn't really have much truck with jumpers. It was lovely, though, a pale heather colour that suited her red hair, and a round neck, and the lambswool felt cosy. Concentrate on the small things, she told herself. She had been reading rather too many self-help books. They were not helping, particularly.

Mrs Offili joined her, looking slightly more cheerful. She was going abroad for Christmas; her parents still had their old house in Antigua. Maggie couldn't have been more jealous.

'Do they have much singing in this?' she asked, a little confused, as the music teacher sat down at the piano.

Mrs Offili blinked, then laughed. 'Oh goodness, I'm so used to sitting at the piano, I didn't pay attention. No! It's just talking; the fourth-formers can sing the songs. I'll play the intros, but not till we get there. Well, that's a relief. Teenage girls auditioning to sing can be highly stressful this early in the day.'

'I know,' said Maggie.

Fleur Parsley the drama mistress, arrived ten minutes late as usual, swinging her long blonde hair from side to side. Despite there being not much difference in their ages – and something of a shortage of younger women to befriend at the school – Fleur and Maggie's approaches to teaching were quite different, and they had never seen eye to eye.

Needless to say, all the girls utterly adored Fleur with her laid-back, casual style and thrilling stories of the many auditions she had nearly passed to get on television.

The first person on the list was Simone, who sidled in looking apologetic about being there as usual. Maggie smiled encouragingly.

'Hello, Simone.'

She made a mental note to see if there was anything to be done about the girl's confidence. Simone had been doing so well last year, but Maggie had noticed – you really couldn't not – that the girl had 'developed' rather dramatically over the holidays and it was obviously causing her some embarrassment. She wondered whether to have a word with her about bra fittings. Maybe she'd just drop a line to her mother. That was not a conversation to look forward to, on any level.

One of the goals of the school was to turn out confident – though ideally not insufferable – girls who could hold their own in institutions and situations governed by men, unafraid to speak up and say their piece. Simone probably had more to say than most as well. Maggie would love to know how to instil confidence in a teenager before she'd entirely managed to instil it in herself, but she'd give it a go nonetheless.

Fleur glanced down the list of characters, frowning slightly.

'Is there a part you had in mind?' she said ominously, looking Simone's new body up and down in a way that Maggie did not like.

'Well, I thought ... maybe Kay?' said Simone, her voice wobbly.

Fleur smiled that beautiful smile of hers.

'Well, that's really ... it's more that the character is meant to be a boy. Like, more of a petite kind of a person,' she said, so charmingly that it would be impossible to take offence until it was too late to think of a response.

Simone coloured instantly and unattractively.

'That would be fine,' said Maggie quickly, trying as ever to control her temper and not entirely succeeding. 'Simone can play pretty much anything.'

'Or the queen?' added Simone in an unconvincing voice.

Fleur paused just a second, then nodded her head imperiously. Maggie felt like kicking her.

Simone turned into profile and intoned, by heart:

'You look cold, are you not? Come, kiss me, child. And I will take you to a place ... a great castle, with towers of ice glittering like diamonds, amid mountains of piercing glass; in a blanket of softest white, with geese as pale as the dawn and waters as hard as iron, and lakes as smooth mirrors, and everything in silence, and you shall not be cold there. Or: you shall be cold, but you shall not mind.'

'Shall I climb aboard?' read in Mrs Offili.

'Come, rest yourself beneath my bearskin coat – would you like to fly as reindeer fly, and land from cloud to cloud?'

'Yes!'

'Kiss me once more on my forehead, my dear child.'

'But you feel so cold ...'

'Ah, living boy. Come fly to the land of marvels with me. I promise, you will not mind.'

Simone's deep voice worked well with the text, and her body stretched up as she spoke. Maggie was pleased. If only she could do that well the rest of the time. Maybe that was the answer: Snow Queen training.

'Mmm, right, thanks, we'll let you know,' said Fleur, and Maggie grimaced yet again. She didn't like it when Fleur did her professional auditioning act, even if her point, made with wide cornflower-blue eyes and a sweet expression, was that that was what it was like out there. Given that very few of Maggie's third years were interested in actually becoming actresses, she didn't really find it very helpful, but it wasn't her department.

'Well done,' she said, smiling brightly. Simone blinked several times, then walked out, hunched over to hide her bosoms. Maggie sighed.

Next in was Alice, who, as usual, over-emoted everything wildly, but with her tossing dark hair, and with the Cornish autumn having all but washed out her golden summer suntan, she certainly looked the part.

'Excellent, Alice,' said Fleur, who had favourites. Alice nodded as if this was simply to be expected.

Felicity crept in, as usual looking unsure whether she actually wanted to be there or if she was just tagging along because it was what all her friends were doing. But her slender boyish frame and slightly hesitant tone made her actually a very good fit for Kay, and all three of the teachers made a mental note.

The rest of the year group followed, with varying degrees of competency. Fortunately there was a part for everyone, from princesses down to old ladies. Eventually, when it was almost lunchtime, Maggie checked the changing room one last time. Sitting there looking awkward was Ismé.

'Hello,' said Maggie. 'Are you ready to come in?'

'Is it compulsory?' Ismé said sullenly. Maggie wondered why she hadn't just asked someone. Uh-oh. That wasn't a good sign.

'The prep is,' she said. 'The auditions aren't. But everyone is going to have a part, and if you audition, you've got a much better chance of not having to be a bystander or whatever.'

Ismé shrugged.

'I haven't prepared anything.'

Maggie blinked.

'Well, that's not ... '

She sighed and decided to tackle it head on, even though it was Sunday, and this was only the Christmas show. The problem was, they had to be consistent. It wasn't fair to show one level of expectation to one group of students and a different one to another.

'That's not acceptable, Ismé. That was the prep from Miss Parsley.'

'Yeah, well,' said Ismé.

'I don't want to have to put you in detention,' said Maggie genuinely.

Fleur came out to see what the problem was.

'Oh, hi, Ismé!' she said brightly. Obviously Ismé, being beautiful and cool to boot, was going on Fleur's favourites list.

'Ismé hasn't done the prep,' said Maggie, feeling ridiculous.

'Well, I'm sure ... I mean, it's a new experience being here, isn't it?' said Fleur, diving into complicity.

'Even so,' said Maggie.

There was a silence.

'Well, I'm sure we can overlook it just this once,' said Fleur. Maggie suspected – rather, she knew for a fact – that Fleur did not overlook things like this with the less favoured. But she opened the door anyway and ushered the girl in.

Ismé looked around, not knowing where to stand, and Maggie couldn't avoid a painful stab of remembrance. It was so strange, coming from the normal world to this place with its weird rules and arcane language and mad stuff they made you do.

'Just go over there,' she said, 'and read off the sheet.'

Ismé casually picked up the first sheet she found lying

on the chairs; she hadn't even brought anything with her. It happened to be Simone's speech.

As soon as she started, Maggie bit her lip to stop a smile spreading over her face. Well, dammit. The girl was great. Her strong London accent seemed to sharpen up – the influence of English baddies in Hollywood movies, no doubt – but it suited the character absolutely fine, and she struck a pose, her glorious hair tumbling behind her. If only she'd done the prep, she could have been fantastic.

'Okay, thanks,' Maggie said when she had finished. 'We're pinning the list up later.'

'Is that it?' said Ismé.

'For now,' said Maggie. 'But in the future, if you could prepare better . . . '

Ismé looked as if she hadn't heard and didn't care, and strolled out of the auditorium.

'Well, she's great,' said Maggie, smiling.

'I know, but she barely lifted the paper,' pointed out Mrs Offili.

'I know,' said Maggie. 'We'll put her in one of the smaller speaking parts. Just to get her going. Try and encourage her to try out for a lead in the summer—'

'Not white enough for the Snow Queen?' said Fleur, instantly. 'Is that what you think?'

'What?' said Maggie, genuinely astounded. 'Of course not. She's brilliant. I just wasn't sure how much she wanted to do it and whether we shouldn't coax her in gradually.'

'Because she's "different"?' said Fleur. 'I happen to think she'd be a marvellous Snow Queen.'

'Well, yes . . . ' started Maggie. 'Well, yes, of course, so do I. But she didn't do the prep, and everyone else did, and it wouldn't be fair. The other girls would think it was off.'

She thought for a second about how the other girls hadn't told Ismé about the audition; hadn't helped her out. She'd put her in that dorm partly because they had a space, but also because she knew Fliss and Simone were kind sorts, and Simone in particular could do with an extra friend; Maggie always felt like she tagged along a little with Fliss and Alice. The fact that they weren't gelling was worrying. And she wasn't the least bit sure that parachuting Ismé into a plum role straight away would be the best thing for her.

'I mean, I've always approved of colour-blind casting,' said Fleur, tossing her long blonde hair. 'That's when—'

'I know what it means,' said Maggie drily. 'I'm just saying she shouldn't have a main role.'

'Yes, I hear you,' said Fleur.

Maggie was furious, but she knew that one of her great failures was always to jump quickly to anger, and she tried to calm herself down.

'Fine,' she said, taking a deep breath. 'Cast her. It goes against everything, but . . . '

'I'm sure I can work with Isma,' said Fleur, putting her pen down in a final way.

'It's Ismé,' said Maggie, standing up. 'Well, if you're sure . . . I'll go through the text in class, you can direct. So I guess your decision is final.'

'I'll write out the cast list,' said Fleur. 'Your handwriting isn't the easiest!'

And she tinkled her beautiful laugh and Maggie decided to see if Claire wanted to go for a pub lunch. She wouldn't – she thought pubs were the filthiest places on God's earth – but Maggie might manage to persuade her if she promised to let her light her Johnny Halliday memorial candle later.

Chapter Two

One bottle of wine and a cheese platter later (Claire wouldn't admit it, but she had something of a taste for British cheese, even if she still hadn't found a British man she liked), the two of them wandered back up the hill to Downey House.

A fog had descended, making them stumble into things and giggle, and Maggie had almost cheered up. She decided to look in on prep on her way upstairs just to check how everything was going, and felt the atmosphere immediately.

Alice, cast as the frog princess, a small midway role, was absolutely furious, first off. Felicity as Kay was rather taken aback and didn't quite know what to say; Simone was perfectly happy with narrator; and Carmen, a cheery soul from one of the other classes, would make a fine Gerda. But it was Ismé's name that Alice had the problem with.

'She's just got here! She didn't learn the prep! You don't just swan in and take the biggest part. That's swanking.'

'Maybe she's just ... really, really good,' said Fliss, trying to cheer her up. It was Sunday too, which meant hot chocolate in the refectory in Christmas term.

'That's not the point,' said Alice. 'Now she'll just get all stuck up. I've been told I'm good enough to audition for drama school. Now I won't get enough stage time and everything will be absolutely crap!' She made a dramatic face. 'It's *so* unfair.'

'It is,' said Fliss loyally.

'It'll still be fun, us all in it,' said Simone encouragingly.

'I'm barely in it at all!' said Alice.

Maggie had popped her head round the door frame.

'Everyone all right? Where's Ismé?'

The girls looked at each other guiltily and Maggie twigged that something was wrong.

'What's the matter?' She stepped forward. 'Is there a problem in your dorm?'

'No, Miss A-dair,' they chorused.

'Good. Make sure there isn't.'

She fixed Simone with a direct stare, and the girl turned pink immediately.

'Simone, you in particular should know what it's like to arrive here not knowing anybody and new to the school. I hope you're all being suitably understanding.'

The girls looked sullen. Oh, fourteen, thought Maggie, and decided to leave them to it.

The girls trooped back to the dorm room after supper to find Ismé on her bed, Skyping someone on her laptop. She immediately shut the lid.

'Well done on the show,' said Simone.

Ismé looked up, exaggeratedly slowly.

'What?'

'*The Snow Queen*. The cast list is up. You got the main part.'

Ismé furrowed her brow. 'Oh, really? I didn't check.'

'It's been up all afternoon,' said Alice.

'Well, nobody told me.'

'Congratulations,' said Fliss. 'You're the Snow Queen.'

Ismé's lip curled.

'Christ. How boring.'

Fliss cast her eyes quickly to Alice, but Alice looked as composed as ever.

'Well,' she said. 'I'm sure you don't have to do it. I don't know if anyone has ever refused, but . . .'

Ismé sighed wearily.

'Oh well, if this prissy place needs you to follow everything to the letter, I suppose I have to.'

There was silence in the room. Fliss felt furious all of a sudden. How dare this girl dismiss everything they did; their entire lives?

'You don't have to be here, you know,' she said. 'There's plenty of people who'd give their right arm to be in a place like Downey House.'

Ismé turned on her, eyes flashing.

'Of course I have to be here,' she growled. 'Because the way the system is set up, this is the only chance I'll get. Or would you rather I went back and cleaned your houses?'

'Nobody said that,' said Alice.

'No, that's because you never think about it. At all,' said Ismé. And she picked up her phone and was clearly typing incredibly loudly about them all, and when Simone looked later, she'd blocked them all on Instagram, which even timid Simone knew was a declaration of war.

Chapter Three

'Look, I just think you should give in on this issue.'

At Phillip Dean Comprehensive Secondary, Barry Frise was having a bad morning. Even worse than normal. There seemed to be a lot of mail on his desk, and his administrator hadn't turned up for the fourth day in a row, claiming post-timetable stress, which required a doctor's letter, but how you would find another letter among all the junk already swamping the office was something of a mystery. And now his new hire was giving him grief.

'No,' said David.

Mr Frise sighed.

'They need their phones.'

'They *don't*. In France you can't take your phone in to school. In independent schools you can't. I think it's absolute craziness to be allowed access to a total distraction machine while you're meant to be learning how to concentrate. You will never learn how to concentrate; how could you?'

'We are a different generation,' said Mr Frise airily.

David shook his head.

'No. Learning worthwhile things is difficult. Has always been difficult. Which means that dinging every two seconds in the classroom is simply horribly unfair on every child involved.'

Mr Frise thought what it would be like to have to try to recruit another English teacher and had the brief sensation of wanting to burst into tears. This was not an unusual situation for him, and he managed to swallow it down fairly fast.

'Well, they're boycotting.'

'Well, they can't. Threaten exclusion; that should bring in some of them. Then I have a few ideas . . .'

Which was how, the following week, first period, David had seventeen pupils traipsing into his class; rather more than half, which was encouraging, all of whom placed their phones in the box provided. Threats were the first level.

He remembered, once again, Maggie's advice. If home is difficult, school can be a respite. Teenagers want to conform; they want to conform to what everyone is doing, and will learn from what everyone else is doing.

Oh why couldn't he stop thinking about her?

He smiled at the class as if nothing had happened, and pulled out a large bag from beneath his desk, handing out brand-new colourful jotters and nice expensive pens to everyone there.

You would think that cool teenagers would scoff at such studious gifts; but they did not. They were, on the whole, thrilled, and David remembered that even though some of them were taller than him, they were of course still children at heart. Also, who didn't like getting new stationery, really?

He was taking them off curriculum completely and, in another trick he'd gleaned from Maggie, had brought out *Brother in the Land*, the most frightening post-apocalyptic book he'd ever read. Below what their reading level should be, of course, but all the better for that. He'd also brought copies of Carol Ann Duffy, the clearest, funniest poet he knew.

'Okay, settle down,' he said, looking around. One pair

were touching each other up in the back row, and he snapped his fingers and separated them without looking up.

'Right, who's ready for some horrifying fiction?'

He gave them ten minutes to discuss horrible films they'd seen and describe what was frightening about them (he could have done, frankly, without learning about *The Human Centipede*). Then he talked, clearly and rationally, about the use of fear in fiction, starting with fairy tales and moving up through dystopic novels, all the way to *Macbeth*. Then he started them reading aloud.

He couldn't believe what he heard. Many of the boys point-blank refused. Some of those who agreed read haltingly, sounding out words, fingers on the text. David blinked. These children would be allowed to leave school next year. How could this possibly have happened?

He stopped the public reading – he didn't like humiliation in his class – and instead read to them himself before giving them a link to the audio book. Then he set the class a short comprehension exercise, mentally labelled the ones who could possibly sit the exams and tried to figure out a strategy, giving a sigh of relief that his time was about to become so busy he would barely have a second to think about Maggie and what she was doing.

Chapter Four

The problem with Catalogue – or Catz, as the kids called it – was that it was untraceable. That was why people loved it, and were scared of it. The forum had swept Downey House like wildfire over the summer. Essentially TripAdvisor for schools, it contained anonymous comments and reviews about both teachers and pupils, and was as prurient, bitchy and liable to make adults despair as you might expect.

The site was banned; it could not be more banned. Of course, being off limits merely encouraged teens – and it was solely for teens; its eye-popping graphics, impenetrable codes and general ferocity kept away all but the most determined adults, who were generally hunted down and exposed anyway. Cataloguing was outlawed from every school in the country.

So of course it flourished.

An hour of social media a night up until the fourth form was considered more than enough by most of the staff and almost all of the parents at the school. Maggie, to her relief, found that it regulated her too. She didn't like looking at pictures of old school friends on Facebook: the weddings she wasn't invited to and the parties that often had Stan's face looming in the background, particularly as Christmas approached.

So having to lock her own phone away like everyone else was quite useful on the whole. Which meant she hadn't even glanced at it when Miss Starling came down one evening, looking furious. On the other hand, furious was rather Miss Starling's default expression, so she didn't take it entirely seriously to begin with.

'Good evening,' Maggie said, still carrying her pile of marking.

Miss Starling had her arms folded.

'The internet,' she said in a way that implied it was a base pit of degradation. Some days, Maggie thought, she had a point.

'Has it gone off?' said Maggie. Anyone under forty tended to get hauled in as tech support around Downey House. Maggie normally asked Simone to do it.

'Has it what?' Miss Starling obviously had no idea that it could be 'on' or 'off'. 'There's a problem with it,' she said.

'Has it gone down?'

'What? No. There's something on it.'

'There's something on the internet?' said Maggie, increasingly confused.

'Yes. And it has to come off.'

'I don't really ... I mean, what site?'

'It's about one of your girls. That's all I know.'

'Where did this ... where did this come from?'

'Something I overheard in the staff room,' said Miss Starling, going red.

'Are you saying this is gossip?' said Maggie. She really did have a lot of marking to do.

'I'm saying, can you look at the internet and see? I don't do internet.' Miss Starling was very flustered now.

'The whole internet?' said Maggie.

'Thank you,' said Miss Starling. 'We can talk about it in the morning.'

*

114

Crossly Maggie went back into the sitting room and fired up the laptop she had rather hoped to be close to be locking away for the night. She googled the school, but it was the usual mishmash of Wikipedia entries and local news stories, nothing remotely useful. She needed an ally, someone who knew this stuff.

She wandered into the third-year common room and glanced around. Most of the girls were absolutely glued to the television, which was playing *Celebs Go Dating*. There was a faint feeling of disapproval among the staff, but every single girl in the school was obsessed with it and they faced a backlash of unprecedented proportions if they tried banning it, so on it stayed. Maggie had tried watching it to discuss its issues – consent, entitlement and so on – with the girls, and had found herself uncomfortably hooked as well, so she didn't make too much fuss about it.

Some of the other girls were on their phones or iPads; Ismé, Maggie saw, wasn't there. Simone was, but Maggie noticed with interest that whereas the other girls were transfixed by the television show, tweeting about it, remarking on it and obviously having a whale of a time, Simone was sitting bolt upright and cautious, as if she knew she ought to be enjoying it but had absolutely no idea how or why.

'Simone, can I borrow you for a minute?' Maggie said softly before most of the girls had realised she was there.

Simone jumped up with a panicked look on her face.

'It's all right, it's nothing bad,' said Maggie. 'Would you mind helping me on the computer for five minutes? You can say no, I know it's downtime.'

'No, it's okay,' said Simone. On the screen, two young, firm-bodied, suntanned people appeared to be rolling around in the surf. This couldn't possibly be suitable, thought Maggie for the millionth time, then wondered again how she could be getting so old.

Although it seemed to her that Simone followed her out with a modicum of relief.

'Where's Ismé?' asked Maggie in what she tried to make a conversational tone as Simone followed her up the stairs to the turret where the teachers had their rooms.

'Um, in the dorm,' said Simone. 'She likes us to get out when she talks to her girlfriend.'

Maggie gave her a look.

'Is she settling in?'

Simone shrugged.

'I don't know.'

'It's hard when you start,' said Maggie, trying to keep the reproof out of her voice. 'You must remember.'

Simone shrugged again.

'We're trying, miss. She doesn't seem to want to know us.'

'You don't think she wants any friends?'

'Probably.'

'Uh-huh. Could you persevere a little, please?'

'She is quite scary, though,' said Simone. 'Doesn't think we're very ... woke.'

Maggie sighed.

'I know. It is hard to be woke at a girls' boarding school. Why not let her teach you? Ask her for tips?'

Simone went quiet.

'I'll try,' she said eventually, even though the idea of going up to Ismé and asking her for woke tips was so excruciating, only a teacher could ever possibly have thought of it.

Simone sat down in Maggie's sitting room. As a first-former she'd often hidden away, reading Maggie's books, and had always loved it: the worn rug, the old fireplace and the long view over the bay, now glittering under a three-quarter moon. Maggie made them both tea and dug up a couple of chocolate digestives, which gave Simone the awkward, unwanted and entirely correct sensation that Miss Adair was about to ask her to sneak on someone.

'Miss Starling says there's something on the internet about the school,' said Maggie finally, sitting down next to her. 'She overheard it in the staff room and has absolutely no idea what it refers to. I've googled and Facebooked but I can't find it. I am really anxious that this doesn't get out of hand or blow up, so I'm going to ask for your discretion. I've always been able to trust you.'

Simone went pink, flattered to be invited into Miss Adair's confidence. But there was another reason for her blush: she knew exactly what Miss Starling was referring to. And she knew that it was very ugly indeed.

Chapter Five

The drama going on upstairs had completely escaped Dr Deveral, who was having what was intended to be a pleasant drink by the fire with Daniel.

He'd arrived with a slightly wicked grin and a bottle of single malt, which was rather unlike him, and they sat by the fire and caught up. Daniel, who worked at Downey Boys, revealed how much the school was missing David; not just his inspiring lessons and his enthusiasm, but his skilful avoidance of the office politics that consumed many enclosed environments.

'He just headed everybody off,' said Daniel. 'I thought he was avoiding admin. It turns out he was maintaining a strong balance. Dr Fitzroy is turning into some weird right-winger. If we're not careful, he'll bring back caning.'

'I'm sure you're exaggerating,' said Veronica, making a mental note to take Dr Fitzroy out to lunch.

'Only just,' said Daniel. 'He puffs about the place all disapproving.'

'That's just part of getting older,' said Veronica, rolling her eyes.

'I know,' said Daniel. 'But when David was about, he could always make him laugh and shake it off.'

Veronica nodded and thought of someone in her school who hadn't been laughing much either.

'Yes,' she said with a sigh. 'We have a similar situation here.'

Daniel grimaced.

'It's just so embarrassing.' Veronica winced. 'If they'd been pupils, I might have understood. I wish ... I wish it hadn't come to that. I am rather fond of them both.'

Daniel nodded.

'And you couldn't ... '

'Oh, it was out of the question. David nearly got a criminal record for being a terrorist.'

'I can see how that might have been a problem.'

'You haven't heard from him?'

Daniel shook his head.

'No one's heard from him. It's like he's gone into a monastic order.'

'Nothing would surprise me about that man ... although it couldn't be one of those silent orders.'

'No ... Veronica?'

Veronica wished there was something else he could call her; always had. But she didn't say anything, just as she tried never to search his face too hard for traces of the tiny baby she had held in her arms for such a short time.

'Yes?'

Daniel was excitedly pulling papers out of his backpack.

'I ... Well. I've been doing some investigating.'

This was the understatement of the year. Poor Susie had got used to Daniel coming home, kissing the children, then vanishing onto the internet as he tracked down dead ends, learned enough conversational Russian to talk to people on the telephone, sent off for documents to long-forgotten communist archives, and bugged the patient and charming incumbents of the Russian embassy for ship movements and declassified naval files. And now he thought he had something.

It was printouts from something that looked like the Russian equivalent of Facebook, called Vkontakte, which clearly worked in more or less the same way. Daniel got his laptop out too. The printouts didn't show it anything like as well, even though he knew that Veronica preferred a hard copy.

Veronica blinked.

'What am I looking at?'

It was the profile of a youngish man, the usual social media shots: a glossy wife with a lipsticked pout; a cute-looking child; what appeared to be a small apartment.

Daniel blinked. 'Don't you ... Here. Look at it on the screen.'

He opened the laptop, where it was in colour. There was also a little video of the couple playing with the toddler, who was lurching about drunkenly, wearing red trousers. It was practically bald; hard to tell whether it was a boy or a girl.

Veronica watched the video carefully, her attention on the adults not the child. Then she saw it.

'Oh my.' She glanced at her tall, fair son with his pointed chin and slanted eyes. It was not really a British face, not when you studied it closely. She looked back at the screen. Yes. The young man in the video resembled him very much.

Her heart started to beat faster.

'Who is this?'

'Who that is isn't really important,' said Daniel, pointing. In the background of the video, and the photos, sitting on the sofa at the back of the room, was a pair of knees. An unre-markable pair of knees, clad in a pair of unremarkable dark trousers, ending in a pair of old laced shoes.

'I think,' said Daniel. 'I think that might be him.'

Veronica found her hands were shaking.

'What ... what on earth do you mean?' she said.

'The man there. The one who looks a bit like ... Well, Susie thinks ...'

'She's right,' said Veronica. 'He does. A little younger, maybe.'

'Thanks for that.' Daniel grimaced. He was coming up to forty, with three young children, and felt it. Veronica waved her hand.

'You know what I mean.'

They both watched the tiny bit of footage play again. How strange, Veronica thought, that someone's little flat, thousands of miles away, could focus their attention so much.

'So how ...'

'Well, the name is common – there are a lot of people in Russia, they all have three names and there's not that many names to go round. But the age is roughly right.'

'In Salonika?'

'No. A suburb of St Petersburg.'

'Oh. That's not where he was from.'

'People move,' said Daniel with a sideways glance.

'Not in communist Russia they didn't,' replied Veronica.

'Well. This Piotr Petrovich Ivanov has been living in St Petersburg since 1998. Wife deceased.'

Veronica blinked.

'Does it say when they got married?'

Daniel winced. 'I was coming to that. My translating is only Google, though. I might be wrong on all sorts of things ...'

'Uh-huh?'

He cast his eyes down.

'Nineteen seventy-five.'

'Oh,' said Veronica. The year before she'd met him. She sat with her back straight. 'So it's probably not him then,' she said stiffly.

'Well, here's the thing,' said Daniel. 'I mean, it could all be coincidence. And it might not be the right person. But the little girl, there?'

'Who?'

'The baby . . . the toddler.'

Veronica looked again at the red-clad lurching figure in the film.

'Yes?'

'Her name is Veronika.'

Chapter Six

It didn't happen all at once, of course. Not at a school like Phillip Dean.

And it wasn't remotely clear to begin with whether it was going to work at all. But one thing David had found about the school was that as long as he turned up, nobody really cared.

Mrs Capstani was the nominal head of department but she taught as little as possible and spent a lot of time in her office doing admin (in fact, David wasn't strictly fair about Leila Capstani, as he had no idea, coming from the independent sector, just how much admin there was).

Then there was Nareeth, the part-time school nurse, whom David quickly learned to adore as she went over and over again way beyond the call of duty in trying to work with social services and with the children in the care system – inevitably the worst readers and most persistent offenders. This was all new to David, and a rapid and formidable eye-opener about how the state treated the weakest in society, and he was unutterably grateful. And Liz Garden, over in history, was also surprisingly helpful, he found (as well as newly single, which he was utterly unaware of).

Barry Frise let him get on with it, which coincidentally when you were dealing with someone as mercurial as David

MacDonald was almost always the best route, manageri- ally speaking.

So David persisted, laying a trail of breadcrumbs to his classroom every day.

He was always there, after class, early in the morning. His door was always open. He had a motley selection of extra books at all standards for anyone who'd like to borrow one. He kept a large bag topped up with stationery, given out for almost any tiny achievement, and apart from his separate study groups for those sitting exams – where he brought the full rigour and expectation of Downey Boys to every child there – he kept the curriculum as light and interesting and engaging as he could possibly manage. He also turned detentions into reading lessons, a way of allowing the very poor readers to retain a bit of dignity in front of their classmates.

Out went *Tess of the d'Urbervilles* – much as he loved it – and in came *Northern Lights*. Out went Anne Frank and in came *Maus*. He gave a class on Stormzy that was so popular he had to give it again.

Gradually, the children started to show up in greater numbers; to talk less. History and maths joined the phone ban too, which resulted in an excellent night out with the historians and mathematicians, cunningly planned by Liz. David spent all hours at his desk; hadn't put so much as a picture up in his grotty rented flat (he had taken the first place he'd seen, without giving it a second thought. His land- lady, forty-five and divorced, who lived downstairs, cooked and left him a Tupperware most evenings. Unsuspecting, David thought it was part of the rental. The landlady's hopes remained up).

It occurred to him, as Christmas approached – and almost guiltily – that he might almost be … well, if not enjoying himself exactly, not in the pit of despair he'd been in in the summer. Which meant he let his guard down, just a little.

Which was when he made the most terrible mistake.

Jazelle Farrendon had barely hit David's radar when he'd started. After so long in a boys' school, he supposed it was inevitable; he automatically summed up the boys, categorised them – always prepared, of course, to be surprised. But the girls he simply wasn't used to, and treated with the same slightly distant cheer he extended to everyone he met, pupil and adult alike. Pupils liked this and could tell he treated them the same as everyone else. Adults – or rather, women – wondered what it was that stopped him getting close to people.

He was used to the pashes of younger boys on older, but nobody – though Ishmael had tried to warn him – had mentioned the unavoidable pitfalls of being a handsome male teacher in a sea of crazed adolescent female hormones.

The girls at Downey House had always been mad for him, but he'd never taught there and barely noticed. Here, however, the girls were around all day and he became aware that one or two of them were hanging about far longer than lessons permitted; showing up after class. He mentioned it to Mrs Capstani, who went slightly pale and simply said, don't let them in and never, ever be in a room alone with them, which made them sound to David like aliens, but he took the advice and found it saddening but helpful.

Jazelle Farrendon, however, wasn't giving up that easily. She was a slender, mousy girl with a heavy fringe she used to cover up her face. She wore as much black – eyeliner and clothing – as she could get away with, which, as they weren't very tough on uniform, was rather a lot. And she was talented.

David had complimented her on her creative work, which, although very badly spelled, was full of energy and promise; passed on as many books as he could lay his hands on; and, of course, doled out the stationery and encouraging little things he brought in.

And in return, Jazelle started to blossom. She put her hand up more in class; brought back keen book reports; was always wearing lipstick despite the fact that it was nominally banned.

By the time David realised what had happened, it was far too late. He had made a rookie first-year teacher's error – and when it came to girls, of course, he *was* a rookie first-year teacher. He had enthusiastically encouraged Jazelle's energy and intellect, and to an affection-starved fifteen-year-old, that felt very ominously like something else altogether.

David didn't realise until he caught two other girls sniggering nastily, and when he mildly enquired what was up, they pointed to Jazelle, who was leaning, chest out, against the wall, staring at him so hungrily even he couldn't miss it. He winced, and immediately attempted to dial back the enthusiasm and the praise and respectfully keep out of her way.

But unbeknownst to him, it was too late. The damage was done.

Chapter Seven

Maggie was still staring at the computer screen.

'Oh God, not this damn thing again,' she said, as Simone brought up Catalogue. 'I thought we'd blocked it.'

'It's ... I've heard it's not very hard to get round the fire-wall,' said Simone, going pink.

'Seriously?'

Maggie was annoyed. If they could get round the firewall for this, they could get round it for anything. There was, she reflected, probably not a lot of point in adults going head to head with a bunch of teenagers over what they were allowed to look at on the internet. It was unlikely to end in a victory for the oldies.

'I'll mention it to Mrs Radzieki.'

Simone rolled her eyes.

'She knows. She spends half her time trying to make it safer and the other half threatening to denounce us to the People's Republic of China.'

'I didn't even think it would be on here,' said Maggie. 'I didn't think Downey House had this problem.'

'I think all schools do,' said Simone, echoing something she'd heard someone else say.

'Ugh, it's like cockroaches,' said Maggie as the bright

yellow and white home page came up. 'Incredibly difficult to eradicate once you've started.'

With a horrible sense of impending doom, Simone continued typing. She wondered if she could delay the process. She didn't want to see it again, see the ugly words.

There were sections for schools, for teachers – Maggie didn't even want to think; couldn't imagine clicking on something so potentially awful. Although it might be nice to know what they thought of you ... No. Definitely not. She turned her gaze away.

'There's loads of them,' she said, leaning over. 'I can't wade through all this. Do you know what people are talking about, Simone?'

Simone, bright puce now, nodded. Maggie found herself getting angry. This entire thing was just a pure and utter crap show, no doubt about it. They spent so much time trying to strengthen their young women, only for this kind of thing to pop up.

She folded her arms as Simone clicked on 'Downey House third form', then scrolled down until she came to a picture – unflattering, a horrible angle, obviously taken unawares – of Ismé. The subject heading was *SNO QUEEN???!!!!* And underneath came a stream of anonymous comments in different colours, each more vitriolic than the previous one. Nasty, vicious, racist comments.

The blood in Maggie's veins ran cold. She didn't even want to read the ongoing stream of filth; it was the kind of thing you'd see in the comments section of a right-wing newspaper.

She turned to Simone.

'You knew about this?'

She realised immediately this wasn't fair.

'Does everyone know?'

Simone nodded.

'Why didn't you tell the staff?'

Simone shrugged. What good would it do Ismé – who had given absolutely no sign of having seen any of it – to have it dragged up around the entire school?

Maggie stared at it.

'I'll speak to Mrs Radzieki in the morning. It's disgusting, this stuff. Utterly, utterly disgusting, and when I find the people behind it . . . This is going to be expulsion level.'

Simone nodded.

'Can you keep it to yourself for now?' said Maggie. Something struck her. 'Have you . . . have you had any?' she said. Simone shrugged.

'A little bit,' she said. 'Nothing like Ismé, though.'

'You know it's all poisonous rubbish?' said Maggie. 'You know to ignore it?'

'Poisonous rubbish is still out there, miss,' said Simone. 'It's still what people think.'

And Maggie, dumbfounded, couldn't think of anything to say to that.

Chapter Eight

Claire had gone to bed, but Maggie stayed up, horrified that a snake had crept into their world. She thought of every girl in the school; those smooth, lovely faces.

She could see them being cruel occasionally, just like all teenagers could be; thoughtless, frightened, and yes, forming cliques. All of that was normal. But they were usually so careful, these days, about respecting race and gender: often tiresomely so. So to see words like this ...

It wasn't as if Ismé was the only non-white girl in the school; far from it. There were plenty of girls of different heritage, many from London, a handful from Nigeria, India and China. And she was hardly the first scholarship girl. It was very puzzling.

It couldn't be the play, could it? Maggie couldn't imagine the casting attracting such approbation. But when she looked at the timings of the messages, it was as if a little gang had got together and said all the most awful things they could think of, only they had typed them out and put them online, where they would sit for ever.

She made more tea. She had no idea how she was going to sleep tonight. She'd speak to Marzia Radzieki in the morning, get the site blocked. Announce it at assembly. There must be ways of tracing these things – although she remembered something she'd read in the paper about the site being encrypted, which meant the perpetrators would be impossible to track down.

She was going to shut down the laptop, at least. Take a book to bed. She glanced, briefly, at the tempting, clickable line of her own name. There was even a star rating next to it. Four. Four out of five.

No. Absolutely not.

She looked at it again. Did that mean lots of fives and a one, or all fours ...?

No.

She went and got changed into her pyjamas, and something else occurred to her. Of course, it was wrong. Well, it wasn't, not really. She was just saving herself the bother of asking. That was all. No biggie.

There were absolutely loads of teachers called David McDonald. Loads. But Maggie couldn't help noticing with a wry smile that most of them were in Scotland. Argyll. Campbeltown. Arbroath. That would have been horribly ironic, she thought. If he'd moved to Glasgow.

No. Of course not.

She ran her eyes down. There it was.

Phillip Dean Comprehensive Secondary School, Darne, Devon. He was forty-five minutes away. At Phillip Dean, of all places. That was the bogey school Miss Starling used to threaten the girls with if they wouldn't behave. Teaching English. She could walk out of this room right now, walk over to her little Mini, step in. Drive away. Give up everything she had.

But for what? For someone who had not even contacted her. Who had walked away – from what? From nothing – leaving her with a broken relationship, a cancelled wedding. And after all, he had always known where *she* was.

Oh, she wished she hadn't searched for him. Not knowing where he was – halfway round the world; up a mountain somewhere – that she could just about manage; that she could deal with. Knowing exactly where he was but knowing she couldn't go to him, or what response would greet her – that was torture.

She went to shut the web page down.

Before she did, she clicked on his star rating. There wasn't anything; he was obviously too new there. She quickly clicked it up to five. Then she slammed the laptop shut before she could think any more about it.

She didn't think she would get much sleep that night. And she was absolutely right.

Chapter Nine

Maggie spent the next morning yawning, with dark circles under her eyes. She'd drunk three cups of coffee, but they hadn't seemed to have any effect; had just made her feel more weird and upside down.

She'd had terrible dreams of computers and spite and David mixed up in it all, and felt herself waking every hour, unable to stop her stomach churning with anxiety. Eventually she'd given up and run herself a bath and taken a book in while waiting for the dawn that came so late, then struggled back to bed to grab a quick ninety-minute nap and now felt like she'd been hit on the head with a solid object.

After breakfast, she'd gone to see Marzia, the ICT head, who had looked into the thread but confirmed what Maggie had already suspected: it could have been done anywhere by anyone, as that was how the site worked. But judging from all the specific details about the play, it was very likely to be someone within the school.

Maggie had been expecting this, but she sighed nevertheless as Marzia took screen grabs of the pages for evidence, checked and tightened the security settings and deleted all the posts.

'There must be more we can do,' she said.

'Well, you could send it to a forensic lab,' said Marzia. 'But it wouldn't be cheap and I don't know how much more they could tell you.'

'What about putting CCTV on the library computers?'

They looked at each other.

'Oh my God, has it come to this?' said Marzia.

'I don't know.' Maggie sighed.

'You look tired,' said Marzia.

'You don't know the half of it,' Maggie told her.

Then it was time to find Ismé. She wasn't at breakfast, which made Maggie very anxious indeed. She peered through a crack in the open dorm door, and saw her sitting in her yoga pose in the empty bedroom. She knocked.

'Can I come in?'

Ismé slowly opened her eyes and looked at Maggie coolly.

'Do what you like,' she said.

But she wasn't fooling Maggie. The girl's composure was fake; she had red eyes and a slight tremble in her hands. Maggie shut the door behind her.

'We know about the website,' she said. 'And don't worry. We're going to get to the bottom of this.'

'But why?' said Ismé, her immaculate facade cracking.

'Jealousy,' said Maggie briskly. 'You're beautiful, you're cool, you're smart enough to get a scholarship and you can act . . . I'm jealous of you, and I'm supposed to be a grown-up.'

Ismé looked genuinely surprised.

'But everyone here is so rich and knows everything and how to get by . . .'

Maggie stared out of the window.

'Nah,' she said. 'They're faking it just as much as anybody else. Posh people are just better at pretending.'

'They all know each other.'

'Yes, well, you knew everyone at your last school. That's normal.'

134

'They all go skiing together and to the Caribbean and stuff.'

'Yes, I know. That's not normal. But it doesn't make them better than anyone else.'

Ismé blinked.

'It's strange,' Maggie said. 'Let me tell you. I've worked with very rich kids and very poor kids. And the pattern of neglect is almost identical. There are girls here who never see their dad because he's always away working, or the parents are on their third marriage. There's as much unhappiness here as there is anywhere.'

Ismé sniffed.

'Did you know,' said Maggie, as something occurred to her, 'in the scholarship fund, there's money for parental visits.'

Ismé looked up.

'What do you mean?'

'Well, if your mum wanted to come and see you. That's covered by the scholarship.'

The yearning on Ismé's face was so great, she looked about five years old. Then she shook her head.

'She works in a bar at the weekend.'

'Well, choose any couple of days. We'll work something out.'

Ismé nodded.

'Okay. Thanks.'

Maggie sighed.

'I'm going to speak to everyone about it.'

'Oh, great. So everyone that hasn't already seen it will go and look.'

Maggie paused.

'I realise that's possible. But we've taken it all down. I don't need to mention your name, and you don't need to come to the assembly.'

'I'm not,' said Ismé.

'But we'll be making it clear that not only is it not acceptable, but we'll be tracking down the person who did it and instant expulsion is on the cards. We'll get them, Ismé. Eventually.'

Ismé shrugged and put her headphones back in, and Maggie vowed that she would get to the bottom of it. Then deeply wished she had an idea of how exactly anyone would do that.

Chapter Ten

Maggie stepped forward on the stage as Dr Deveral announced that there was something serious to be discussed. She took a deep breath and looked out over the assembled girls.

'I realise,' she said, 'that you live much of your lives online and that is how things are these days. And I know that it is the job of adults to try and stop you doing and seeing inappropriate things, and that your job is to try and get round these strictures.'

There was some giggling at this, quickly quelled by a sharp glance from the headmistress.

'But,' said Maggie, 'there are absolute lines and you all know what they are. If you are unaware of what is completely and utterly unacceptable in this school, there is a booklet sent to you and your parents, which I am also going to make you all read and write a report on this week.'

Miss Starling made it clear from her facial expression how unacceptable she personally found this, for it would get in the way of other prep, but Maggie was unbending.

'I am not going to dignify what happened with a discussion of the site,' she said. 'The guilty parties know exactly who they are and what they did. We are going to find out who was responsible for this,' she went on, 'and it is going to be treated as seriously as we are able. We do not accept bullying at Downey House. We will not have it. We will find you, and when we do, your time here will be over.'

Everyone went silent. Maggie looked around the hall, satisfied that she'd impressed the seriousness of this on everyone. The first years were wide-eyed in horror. Then she simply nodded and turned her back, and assembly was over.

In class, however, she found it hard to concentrate. The messages seemed more likely to have come from people who had met Ismé; found her perhaps a little cool or prickly. People involved with the Christmas show, quite probably. That meant it was most likely someone among her own third-formers.

She glanced around the class anxiously. It couldn't be Astrid Ulverton, surely, a highly talented musician who could barely be separated from her beloved clarinet. Simone Pribetich; surely not. Barb was completely uninterested in anything that wasn't lacrosse or talking about horses; Maggie couldn't imagine how she'd get up the enthusiasm.

Alice Trebizon-Woods – well, she could certainly be cutting enough to say something cruel, but she couldn't imagine Alice stooping so low as to troll someone. That just wasn't her style. Plus the appearance of a Trebizon-Woods in the library was something the librarian would have been unlikely to forget. Felicity Prosser? She was so sensitive about everything, Maggie simply couldn't imagine her using racial slurs.

It was an absolute puzzle. She couldn't bear to think that any Downey girl – any student who had ever been in her care – would be capable of doing such a thing. But she knew this was bias; that people did do horrible things on the internet, every single second of the day.

She taught a little about myth and legend, set them some Angela Carter and then brought out a Helen Dunmore poem at the end to discuss imagery and also an idea she felt was currently important: that if you behaved like a bad person, whatever your intentions, it was entirely possible that you would become one.

Chapter Eleven

There was a card pushed under his door. With love hearts. David looked at it, sighed, binned it, redoubled his efforts to try and make his classroom a place of serious, committed work with a fun side. He poured everything into it. He also took Jazelle aside at the end of class. She was wearing leggings – technically the school uniform was black trousers, which could be worn by both boys and girls, but these were sprayed on and alarmingly revealing – and heavy make-up, and had half unbuttoned her blouse. She looked incredibly excited to be there. It was getting worse and worse, and he had to say something.

'Jazelle,' he began sternly. He wasn't used to doing this, and hated to be unkind. 'There has been some talk around the school.'

That was putting it mildly. Several of the boys had told him up front exactly what Jazelle had in mind, and it broke his heart that this was a discussion boys and girls had publicly, without the remotest consideration of the emotional impact it could have on those involved.

'I have to ask you to stay away from my room apart from for lessons, and certainly don't send me anything. You're a clever and special girl, and I do understand that, but it's just inappropriate and wrong. I don't want to take it further, but I will if I have to. Do you understand?'

The girl's heavily mascaraed eyes began to well up, and David immediately regretted his naivety at not calling the school nurse in at the same time. He was about to suggest Jazelle paid a visit there when she turned on her heel and fled.

Angry at how he'd handled the situation, dropped even further off the radar of his long-suffering friends, he walked for miles, with Stephen Dedalus his only companion, through the horrible back estates of the worst side of town. Sometimes he would go down to the docks, watch the big, dirty military ships come and go; wonder on some level if he shouldn't just jump on one, wherever it was headed; start over, a new life.

Then he thought of the children. He couldn't abandon them. He'd have to adjust. The one thing he hadn't noticed was that through everything, attendance had remained high. His fun approach had tempted them in, and now he gradually led them onwards, becoming more pointed, serious and, as always, incredibly clear. He was used to his lessons being well attended, didn't realise how rare it was. Some students were arriving for his classes, then hunking off for the rest of the day. Now that the children had decided he was all right – which he'd accomplished with his open door – they were happy to attend.

He took everyone through the lesson at the pace of the slowest learners – which could be very slow indeed – then emailed out extra work for those he felt could stretch to it, for them to return via email too. With empty evenings to fill, he marked their papers incredibly thoroughly, full of helpful hints and tips and suggestions for extra reading.

What felt like failure to David was, in fact, very quietly turning into success, and the marks were rising.

And then Ofsted showed up, and everything immediately got worse.

Chapter Twelve

David had never had to deal with Ofsted before. Everyone else had, and they were charging about in a panic. The school was already in special measures; one more bad inspection and Barry Frise knew he was going to lose his job and they were going to send in some scary super-head, or close the school and bus everyone out to different places, none of which wanted them, which meant fights, police presence and worse.

Barry asked David to come and help with the playground litter pick-up and he agreed immediately, checking that there'd be lots of teachers there with the kids. Barry squinted at him. No, there'd be no children. Just teachers.

'That's ridiculous,' said David. 'Why can't they pick up a bit of litter?'

'They're scum, some of them,' said Barry bitterly. 'They'll start kicking everything over and screaming and hitting each other with it.'

'Are you sure?' said David. 'Isn't it worth a shot? If you treat them as useless, I'm sure they'll live down to your expectations.'

'Ah yes, I forgot the *Guardian*-reading privately educated contingent was here,' said Mrs Capstani, rolling her eyes.

David, furious, marched into his next class; a group that

he was having read out *Animal Farm* very slowly in order to help those who still limped over their words.

'Right,' he said. 'Someone said something to me today that I didn't believe. We're cleaning up the school grounds. And apparently you guys don't know how to clean up after yourselves, is that right?'

'My mum says so!' shouted Lee Afton, whose shorn hair and diminutive stature made him look about nine years old, and who compensated for this by a ferocity in fighting that scared even the senior boys. There was class laughter.

'Okay, well, I disagree. I'm telling all my classes to turn up for litter pick-up,' said David. 'This afternoon. It'll be good for the school, and good for you.'

There was massive booing. David was absolutely dumbfounded.

'Honestly? Do you really like the place being a total state?'

There was a variety of shrugging. Foresta Jenkins in the front row folded her arms.

'That's all you think we're good for, innit?' she said, staring at him. 'Just get us in training, eh?'

'If we're lucky we might get a job on the bins, right?' said someone else.

'Yeah, or be cleaners,' added Foresta.

David stared back.

'Of course not,' he said. 'Although I do think any work is good work if it's done well. But this is nothing to do with that. This was just an idea to come together to do something good.'

'We've had enough of do-gooders,' said another kid, and various people agreed.

David blinked. This had simply never occurred to him.

'But you're not doing it for you,' he said. 'You're doing it to make the school nice.'

'School ain't nice,' said someone else.

'You see, the thing is . . . ' began David. And he did something he had absolutely been forbidden to do.

Most schools, as soon as they learned (normally twenty-four hours in advance) that they were having an Ofsted visit, informed the parents, asked the students to dress smartly and told them that some of them would be interviewed. This worked well. In most schools.

At Phillip Dean, Barry Frise had decided to go a different way. He wasn't going to tell anyone.

His reasoning was this: the kids would show up, treat it as a great laugh and behave as badly as they possibly could, goading every teacher in the hope that they would crack, shout and then get into serious trouble. They would then take the inspectors aside and repeat scurrilous rumours.

Barry's plan was to get the place as clean and tidy as possible – on the teachers' hours – show the inspectors the new chemistry equipment that he'd actually ordered the previous year but hadn't put in the labs yet in case the children used it all as weapons, and hope that the incredible arse-ache and paperwork that would be involved in closing the school and moving the children would somehow put them off doing so.

He'd also announced at morning assembly that there would be no taking of the register the following day as they were doing a register audit. This was a totally meaningless phrase, but he hoped it would allow some of the more persistently naughty to realise that it would be a very good day indeed to bunk off.

David might never have been through an inspection before, but he was up to date with the procedure, and absolutely furious that Barry thought so little of the children. This culture of low expectation was helping absolutely nobody.

'There's an inspection tomorrow,' he said now. Someone made a 'woo' sound. 'If we fail,' he continued, 'it might mean

144

the school being shut. Some of you will be sent to St Patrick's, some out of the district altogether.'

'St Patrick's is evil,' someone said.

'It could disrupt your exams; it could mean you having to get bussed in and out every day.'

'Would you lose your job, sir?' asked someone else.

'Well, yes,' said David. 'But it's you guys who are important. Your futures.'

'Our futures in cleaning up?'

'I'm afraid so,' said David. 'All adults have to clean up. It's just the way of it. But I think you can do more than that. Honestly I do.'

He let that sit there.

'Anyway, I'm going to cheat tomorrow. I'm going to show off. Who's up for a musical lesson?'

There were some tentative smiles.

'I'm going to pretend to be trendy,' said David. 'There might be Stormzy.'

There were groans.

'Stormzy is SOOOOO over'

'Ugh, I never get it right,' said David. 'Okay. I'm bringing oldies. It will make a change. Duluth, can you start reading from the top, please?'

That freezing December afternoon, there weren't a lot of them – not a majority by any means. But even so, David was absolutely surprised and delighted by how many pupils did, in fact, come and join the litter pick-up, despite the cold wind coming off the Channel, and the fact that everyone else had gone home.

Chapter Thirteen

Maggie was a little nervous about the first rehearsal, after all the kerfuffle. Fleur Parsley, on the other hand, bounced in full of excitement.

'Now, my team,' she said conspiratorially.

Maggie glanced at Ismé. She was standing aside, not chatting to the rest of the third-formers. Who did she suspect? Worse: did she believe that more than one of them had used those ugly words? That they were just writing down what everybody else said?

Regardless, she stood there looking graceful in leggings and a long top as Fleur led the room in a series of preposterous breathing exercises, with big exhortations to 'Feeeeeeellll ... relaaaaaaax ... beeeee in the space ... Miss Adair, why aren't you joining in?'

Maggie pointed out that she was just there to help with the text, but Fleur gave her what was clearly meant to be a pitying smile and explained that everyone could do with a little mindfulness, particularly if you were having stress in your life, and how it could really help drain any toxins in your body, and Maggie blinked and didn't mention that she didn't believe in toxins, but instead gamely came forward and pretended to be taking some deep breaths without rolling her eyes too much.

Finally they managed to start. Fliss was so overexcited, she'd learned everybody else's lines as well as her own. Alice told Fleur she was going to improvise, and Fleur said that was absolutely fine, part of the excellent craft of theatre, and Maggie had to step forward and be the bad guy again and explain that there were musical cues and lighting cues to fit in, and the point of the show was learning some decent literature, and Fleur and Alice shared long-suffering looks of creativity stifled.

Ismé was still reading from her script, but as she stepped forward, her poise was absolute; so unusual for a fourteen-year-old girl.

'We have driven well,' she said to Fliss as Kay. *'But why do you tremble? Here, climb into my warm fur and let me kiss thee.'* And she looked Fliss straight in the eye.

Afterwards, Fliss would trace it all back to that moment. She had been desperate, she knew, to meet someone. To fall for someone. Of course she had; they all knew that. Simone had a boyfriend; Alice had suitors, gallons of them. Fliss was just so desperate to fall in love; to experience what she saw in the films, what she heard in the songs and read about in magazines and books. A pure, beautiful love with some-one amazing.

Ismé pulled the blanket they were using as a fur coat around Fliss on the chairs that represented the sleigh.

'Are you still cold?' she read. *'Now you must have no more kisses, or I shall kiss you to death.'*

And Fliss, out of the blue, fell head over heels for her beautiful room-mate.

'Well, I feel that went all right, considering,' said Maggie as she and Fleur compared notes afterwards.

'It was magnificent,' said Fleur, nodding. 'I knew my

instincts were right. I always have good instincts. I should have been a director really.'

Maggie nodded. 'If your instincts are good ... have you the faintest idea who's been poison-penning Ismé?'

For once, Fleur didn't smile, just shook her head seriously. She'd heard.

'It's grim,' she said.

'I know,' said Maggie.

'It used to happen to me all the time, you know,' said Fleur. 'People were just *so* jealous. I mean, obviously I had loads and loads of girlfriends around me, but, you know. Jealousy is a terrible thing. I still get it now.'

Maggie nodded politely.

'Well, keep your ears open,' she said. 'The girls talk to you more than me.'

'They do, don't they,' simpered Fleur. 'I think they feel they can tell me anything. They're more my friends than my pupils really.'

Maggie also felt this, but had a slightly different take as to whether it was a good thing.

'Good. Well, if they do confide in you – even just a word, just a rumour – please let me know.'

'Not if it's breaking a confidence.'

'*Yes* if it's breaking a confidence! You're not a priest!'

'Acting is all about trust,' said Fleur primly.

'Someone is trying to destroy one of our pupils,' said Maggie, hating how defensive she sounded. 'And I'm not going to let it happen. And neither are you.'

Chapter Fourteen

Rehearsals went on, but for Fliss, there was an added dimension. Suddenly she couldn't stop thinking about Ismé. She thought about her as Ismé sat cross-legged, meditating, or Skyping her girlfriend, or sullenly folding her arms in lessons. She thought about the two of them together, and how cool it would be to come out as bi – Fliss was always worried about not being cool enough.

After that first realisation, she had lain awake all evening, alternately horrified and dizzy with excitement. Was she gay? That was quite exciting actually. Or bisexual maybe, as she still fancied Charlie Puth, obviously. Ooh, even better. A thought struck her. Obviously she was playing a boy in the school play. Might she be transgender too? She had always fretted a bit about how uninteresting she was. Well *this* was definitely more interesting. Definitely. Hmm. Maybe she should show people she had a new identity now. Change something about herself.

She propped herself up on her elbow in the dark. She could just see the outline of Ismé lying prone on the bed. She didn't look as if she were asleep either. She was so beautiful, thought Fliss happily. So gorgeous. And there were still three weeks of rehearsals to go.

Maybe the fact that they had to kiss on stage – even if it

was a chaste kiss on the forehead – maybe it could turn into something more.

And with these happy thoughts turning in her head, she sank into a grateful sleep.

The next day she approached Ismé first thing, nervous and blushing.

'Would you like me to help you run through your lines?' she said.

Ismé had never had to learn lines before; there hadn't been anything like that at her school, whereas Downey House had all had enforced poetry recitations since the girls were six years old. She didn't really know where to start.

And she was finding it hard to keep it up, this pretence that everything was fine and that she didn't want to talk to anyone. She hated this school, everyone here and everything about it – as well as the fact that someone, and possibly more than one person, was out to get her, so she mistrusted everyone – but she was absolutely so lonely.

In the evening, she got to log in and talk to her girlfriend Kizzie, and see what all her friends at home were getting up to without her: all the Instagram posts they put up of them having a hilarious laugh; all the Snapchat conversations she was included in but couldn't really keep up with because she didn't know what they were talking about. She couldn't do without it, but it was ripping her apart.

'Yeah, all right,' she sniffed. Fliss was friends with that mega-cow Alice, but she probably wasn't that bad really. She didn't even understand her own privilege, that was how stupid she was. Fliss beamed with joy and Ismé rolled her eyes.

'I'm thinking of cutting my hair,' announced Fliss at breakfast that morning, eating a yoghurt and a piece of fruit, which, while an improvement on last year when she wouldn't eat anything at all, still wasn't exactly as much as her family and friends would have wished.

Simone gasped. She hated her own bushy mop (although, as Zelda had pointed out last year, with the right products to get rid of the frizz, it could be her crowning glory) and thought Fliss's naturally straight, naturally blonde Alice in Wonderland locks were the height of enviability.

'Why? How short?'

'I was thinking pretty short,' offered Fliss. Alice raised an eyebrow.

'Why?'

'I just fancied a change,' said Fliss, doing her best to be mysterious.

'Women only cut their hair under dramatic circumstances,' said Alice, with her usual woman-of-the-world-who-knows-everything demeanour. 'And I don't think you're getting divorced or moving house.'

Fliss shrugged.

'Maybe I'm just getting fed up with a binary world.'

Alice laughed.

'What does that mean?'

In Fliss's head it had sounded grown-up and challenging and fascinating.

'You know. The idea that everything has to be masculine or feminine. Maybe I want to be neither. Or both.'

'What, like one of those frogs they taught us about in biology that changes sex?' said Alice, unable to stifle her giggles.

'But your hair is so beautiful,' moaned Simone.

Ismé was sitting at the end of the table ostensibly reading a book and ignoring them, but now she looked up.

'That's cool,' she said to a flame-faced Fliss. And that was all it took.

Chapter Fifteen

Third-formers were allowed into the village on Saturday afternoons in term time if they weren't going home.

Fliss set out with her friends and a determined expression, having googled 'gamine' several times. She'd attempted to strike up more conversations with Ismé about gender, but Ismé hadn't seemed particularly keen, which hadn't dampened Fliss's ardour at all.

The village was sleepy, but to the girls, penned up at Downey House, it was a hotbed of excitement – the local shop stocked *Vogue* (they knew its clientele pretty well) as well as as much sugar as the girls could physically carry, and very necessary supplies of Nik Naks and Diet Coke, and the tiny pharmacy had an entire wall of Barry M that got emptied more or less every Saturday, along with their supplies of witch hazel.

There was only one hairdresser, who was slightly more used to doing shampoo and sets for the mainly elderly population (as Maggie had once found out to her cost, having gone in to get a few highlights in her luscious red hair and emerging looking rather more like Ginger Spice circa 1995). Fliss felt simultaneously nervous and defiant walking into the salon. That was the thing about having short hair: it simply wasn't done at their school. Even the alternative, emo-type girls had long black hair, or plaits. You could just about get away with a shoulder-length bob if you were, like, a total nerd, but otherwise all the girls had long silky hair; it just came with the territory.

Maggie had often wondered about it – her generation had long hair, short hair, whatever they felt like at the time. This lot seemed like clones to her.

'I want you to cut it off,' Fliss said to the kindly-looking woman standing behind the black chair. 'Short.'

'How short?' said the woman. 'It's such beautiful hair.'

'You should sell it,' said Simone.

'Oh yuck, how gross,' said Alice. 'For skanky extensions for a glamour model?'

Simone suddenly had a ridiculous fantasy of cutting off all her own hair and then attaching Fliss's hair to her head – she'd once seen them do something similar on an episode of *America's Next Top Model* – but decided, blushing, that this was absolutely not the time to mention it.

'Actually,' said the hairdresser, 'you can donate it, if it's not dyed.'

'It's not,' said Fliss.

'It can go to make wigs for kids in chemo.'

If anything was going to make Fliss's mind up, it was this: to be a massively good-doing heroine was simply too amazing an opportunity to resist.

'Great!' she said.

'Do you want me to cut a bit off and you can see what you think, then I can take it shorter if you'd like?'

'No,' said Fliss. 'The wigs won't be as good. Just do it all.'

Alice and Simone stood solidly by, their faces serious. They knew what a bold undertaking it was, as the great fronds of hair – Fliss's mother's pride and joy – tumbled to the floor. There seemed, Fliss thought, to be an awful lot of it. She tried to ignore her beating heart. This was going to be her reinvention. Models did it all the time. Yeah.

After half an hour, during which nobody spoke – with only the hairdresser saying at one point that she was going to turn the clippers on to do the back, which made everyone wince a bit – she was done.

Fliss looked up in the mirror at the tiny immature boy staring back at her, and burst into tears.

Chapter Sixteen

'You look gorgeous!' said Simone immediately. Fliss could actually have grafted a horn onto her forehead and that would still have been Simone's response, but Fliss let it stand.

'Well,' said Alice. 'I don't think you're going to be able to order a drink at a bar.'

The hairdresser stood back with a slightly resentful 'well, that's what you said you wanted' look on her face and crossed her arms. Fliss paid her, head down.

In fact, the haircut suited her very well; it *was* gamine and highlighted her pixie face and neat chin. But it did make her look very, very young. On a more confident person it would have looked utterly tremendous. On Fliss, she looked like she'd done it herself.

Fliss's sister Hattie didn't help. As they arrived back at school, with Simone telling her all the way how brilliant it was, Hattie marched in from the hockey pitch.

'Christ!' she scoffed. 'Well, Daddy did always want a boy.'

Tears rose in Fliss's eyes yet again, and she broke away from the others, pushing through Claire and Maggie, who were heading out for the afternoon.

'*Bah, non, c'est mignonne,*' said Claire, looking after her.

Maggie blinked. 'I like it too,' she said. Then she looked around. 'It's not like Fliss to break ranks. I hope she's not going through one of her phases. Why do all the girls have such long hair anyway? All of them?'

Claire shook her own short shiny bob. 'Eet ees what boys like, *non*?'

'There aren't any boys here! That's meant to be the entire point of the school.'

'Ees Eenstagram ... Kardashian ... porn ... '

Maggie sighed.

'That is so annoying. I think I'll cut my own hair off.'

'No. Do not. Is your best feature,' said Claire and walked on, leaving Maggie staring after her, thinking with some sadness that that was the first compliment anyone had given her in at least six months.

Fliss vanished into the bathroom before she went back to the dorm. She wouldn't be upset in front of Ismé. She wouldn't be. She'd be fine.

She washed her face, and pulled out a small red lipstick she'd bought in the summer. Obviously they weren't allowed to wear make-up in school until fifth form, but it was Saturday after all.

Her hair did look healthy and shiny, even if the back of her neck felt exposed and utterly freezing. She tried the lipstick on. That definitely looked ... Well. Better. Why did her features appear so small and pinched? She hadn't realised how much her long fine hair had been part of her; had never even really looked at her chin before. Was it too pointy? At least it wasn't double, like Simone's, but ...

She sighed in deepest misery. What had she done? What *had* she done? She hated looking at herself in the mirror. Last year it had been her weight. This year ...

She blotted her lipstick. Alice and Simone had gone on into tea, so surely this was her chance to catch Ismé alone.

Heart beating wildly, she walked into the dorm.

Chapter Seventeen

Ismé was sitting at her desk, having an argument with someone over Skype. A girl. This must be the infamous girlfriend, Kizzie. Fliss didn't have time to get anything more than a cross blurred expression before Ismé slammed down the lid.

'Can't you knock?' she hissed.

'Sorry,' said Fliss instinctively, even though it was her room too. Then, 'Are you okay? Was that your girlfriend?'

'It doesn't matter,' said Ismé. 'It's not really anyone's business.'

'I know that,' said Fliss. 'It just sometimes helps to tell someone.'

'Does it?' said Ismé. She turned round. 'You cut your hair,' she said.

Fliss's heart leaped. She'd noticed!

'Well, yes,' she said.

Ismé looked her up and down.

''S cool,' she said.

Fliss went bright red.

'Are you sure? It's a bit dramatic.'

'Stops you looking like everyone else round here.' Ismé glanced at her watch. 'Oh crap. I still haven't even looked at the script.'

Fliss walked over.

'I told you, I can help you read through it. If you like. I know your part.'

Ismé smiled. 'You are keen, aren't you? Aren't you going to have tea?'

Fliss got signed in and out for meals and wasn't allowed to miss one. She shrugged.

'Yeah, whatever,' feeling a small moment of boldness and rebellion inside her.

'I've got some biscuits if you'd like some,' said Ismé carelessly, and that was all Fliss needed to scramble to sit beside her.

The next half-hour, as Fliss helped Ismé with her pick-up lines and edged closer to her on the bed, was blissful.

'Cheers,' Ismé said as they got up to go to the rehearsal together. 'Thanks. I needed that.'

'Is everything okay with ... your girlfriend?' asked Fliss again, trying to keep her tone light, as if it was a simple enquiry anyone might make.

Ismé sighed.

'Oh, usual. Wants me to give it up, move back home.'

'I wanted to do that so badly the first year I was here,' said Fliss. 'I tried to get expelled. On purpose.'

Ismé looked at her once again with those dark, searching eyes, and Fliss realised how much she loved the whole beam of her attention. Oh God, she fancied her so much. *So* much. What would she give to be her girlfriend.

'Did you really?'

'Oh yes. Made a huge stink. Shouted out at the Christmas concert and everything.'

Ismé smiled as they crossed from the main building to the theatre hall.

'You're not at all how you come across,' she said.

Fliss wanted to say at that point that nobody was, but she held her tongue.

'Well, good,' she said. 'I wouldn't want to be one of those stuck-up know-nothings you think we all are.'

To Fliss's immense relief, Ismé smiled at the cheek and rolled her eyes.

'Well, you are that too. But you look like you have the potential to be woke.'

Fliss still wasn't entirely sure what that meant, but she took it as a compliment nonetheless. And that evening, they performed so beautifully together that Fleur was in paroxysms of delight. Maggie, who knew Fliss very well, was slightly more suspicious, but she put the idea out of her mind. Fliss was boy-mad; everybody knew that. It was just nice to see Ismé had made a friend, that was all.

Chapter Eighteen

Still pleased by the success of the litter pick-up – because any success at all counted in this environment, and he was going to celebrate every bit of it – David was even feeling slightly perky as he put on his suit and tie the next day.

The kids teased him about the way he dressed; there were very few male teachers anyway, never mind ones who wore jackets and ties, but David felt that although you could complain a lot about the independent sector, a commitment to smartness and neatness wasn't the worst thing about it, and the kids deserved to be taught by someone who looked like they'd made some effort to be there.

It was a rather lovely day for this late in the year: pale blue skies and a low-lying sun that made drivers hunch over their windscreens. He walked Stephen Dedalus down by the port, then carried straight on, hoping for the best from the inspection.

It started off well almost immediately, as he was greeted by Pat and Liz, two women who had inspected Downey Boys when he'd worked there. Maggie had found them awful, but they'd had a soft spot for David, and he smiled at them happily.

Pat was wearing a tight trouser suit that stretched rather

formidably over her rear end, and was carrying her omni-present clipboard. Her face beamed with pride.

'See! Isn't it better to be getting your hands dirty in a real school?'

'Downey *is* a real school,' said David, but he shook her hand warmly as Barry Frise tried to contain a happy smile at having an ally on his team even before they'd got started.

'Yes, but think of the difference you can make here,' said Pat. 'So sorry to hear about Maggie Adair.'

'What about her?' said David instantaneously, panic gripping his heart. 'Is she all right?'

'Oh, I dunno,' smirked Pat, happy to have gossip some-one else didn't know. 'I just heard there'd been a bit of fuss, that's all.'

The colour drained from David's face. What had hap-pened? Was Maggie still there? Had she left after she got married? What? What?! He couldn't concentrate for a second.

'Well, yes, *quite* the scandal,' said Pat. 'The school seems to be weathering it, just about. Although between the two of us, I never really felt she fitted in there.'

David, who by default tended to like everyone, suddenly remembered why he didn't like Pat very much.

'Would you like to come in? I think there's tea,' said Mr Frise, trying to be charming. Suddenly everyone was swarm-ing around and Pat's attention was distracted.

'And biscuits, I hope,' she said with some feeling. 'Now, that is the one thing you always got at Downey. Amazing biscuits.'

'I'm afraid the school food here is ... up to national stand-ards,' said David, grimacing. He still found the standard of food the children were offered very depressing after the decent, wholesome meals that were served at Downey. Dry pizza or fish fingers and fried potatoes and a miserly amount of damp carrots didn't seem to him to set them up properly at all, particularly when accessorised by a tuck van that waited every afternoon at the school gates and sold nothing but junk and fizzy pop; and a chip shop on the corner doing a roaring trade. He thought it showed in the pupils' skin and their doziness after lunch, but had enough on his hands with the day-to-day work to even start on that one.

'Oh great,' said Pat. 'I love a nugget, me.'

'She does!' said Liz.

'So perhaps you'd like to sit in on David's first class,' said Barry Frise, unable to believe he'd got so lucky. He was terrified of the inspectors and kept having to wipe his hands down his pockets. If he lost the job here – which was very much on the cards – he'd have to go back into a classroom and teach again. Nothing could be worse than that.

'Yes, it will be *very* interesting to see how you cope with children who've been allowed to think for themselves,' said Pat in what she obviously believed to be a flirtatious manner.

David did his best to smile and led them through. He'd offered to take the entire year group, which Barry had fallen on with alacrity, and was now firing up his speakers.

'This won't necessarily be your kind of music,' he told the inspectors. 'But I wanted to do a little bit of compare and contrast. First, the Burns we were looking at ... ' And he started to recite, without dramatic flair, but carefully and clearly, 'A Red, Red Rose'. It was hard, as he read the old Scottish words, not to find himself thinking of somebody else ...

'And now we're going to look at another genius. Both of them, I think, were born pretty special. And I suspect they'd have got on.'

He pressed a button on his iPad and the familiar – to him,

if not to the students – opening chords of Stevie Wonder's 'As' came on.

'*Till all the seas gang dry,*' he recited from the Burns, and then Stevie chimed in with his version of everlasting love.

'*And rocks melt like the sun,*' David read. '*Until the oceans cover every mountain high,*' crooned Stevie.

He let the Stevie Wonder play on, noticing as he did so that the kids were starting to move.

By the end, they were clapping.

'This is all that simile and metaphor is,' said David. 'It's all it's ever been. Trying to put feeling into what's all around us. And to use the music of words. Because emotions never change. Here, listen to this poem – when do you think it was written?'

And he started reciting 'Walk Down That Lonesome Road'.

There were various guesses at the 1700s or 1800s, and they were surprised to find out it was younger than David himself. He played the beautiful Poozies version for them, and many of the kids found themselves surprisingly emotional.

As David took them through the emotions of pain and regret, and how poetry was only an effort to put your rawest, most honest feelings down in a condensed way that got as close as possible to the reality of felt experience, he experienced one of those rare teaching moments when, inspectors be damned, he could *feel* himself connecting.

'We're going to finish with something that I think is pure poetry,' he said. 'It's very old. But I think it's quite something.' And, amazed that so many of them had never heard it before, he played 'Eleanor Rigby'. More than a few of the girls were crying as the bell rang.

'Okay, dismissed,' he said absent-mindedly. It was what he had said at his old school; here, nobody waited two seconds to hear what the teacher might like to say in conclusion.

Except that there had, in fact, been a couple of quiet moments after the bell. At Phillip Dean, this was absolutely a rarity.

Barry Frise glanced over at Pat. She was making what looked suspiciously like ticks on her board, and for the first time in a long time, he felt himself relax.

Chapter Nineteen

The end of term swung round faster than anyone – particularly Simone, who had her head full doing double loads of classes – could believe.

And the school troll still hadn't been found.

'It's ridiculous,' Maggie was saying to Marzia, for the millionth time. 'Why can't we just track them down? I thought that was the whole point of the internet.' Because she'd noticed that even if Ismé seemed to have softened a little towards Fliss, she still wasn't talking to anyone else. Nasty comments continued to be left; it was a dreadful environment for everyone.

In class, Ismé was still confrontational, sighing loudly whenever they read any dead white males, which was unfortunate considering they had a heavy schedule of Shakespeare and Yeats ahead. The other uncomfortable thought was that she was absolutely right: they did have to extend the reading list. They'd managed to work on a lot more Scottish authors at Maggie's old school; there was no reason why Downey House couldn't confront the realities of the world better than it did. That, however, involved changing the curriculum, which involved talking to Miss Starling and that felt a little bit like a conversation Maggie needed to have another day.

Marzia shrugged.

'I know. I'm sorry. Encryption. I honestly thought we'd manage it through checking the library logs, but ... nothing. There's no evidence at all, apart from the fact that it's from round here. I'm so sorry. Normally with this kind of thing someone feels guilty or owns up, but it's weird – with this, nobody seems remotely upset. And I'll tell you the other thing: they don't comment on anything else. Only on Ismé. Not on the teachers, not on the facilities. Just that one girl. Who hardly anybody knows.'

'Which really narrows it down,' said Maggie, completely depressed. 'It must be someone from my form. Nobody else would even care. Oh God, I'm a terrible teacher.'

'This happens,' said Marzia. 'It's just what teenage girls do. Our job is to try and keep them from being less evil than their natural instincts.'

Maggie sighed. It was such a shame. Now that they were into December, the school looked so beautiful. The caretakers always pulled out all the stops at Christmas: there were wreaths everywhere, the large fire in the main hallway was lit throughout the month, and the smell and crackling warmth was welcoming and cheerful; there were concerts and shopping trips and it was one of the nicest times of the school year. Everyone felt it. Normally.

Now it felt poisoned. Even today, when all the parents were arriving for the Christmas show. Outside, the ground was frozen hard with frost, and the snake of cars arriving with proud parents ready to take their children home afterwards was winding up the path.

The dorms were packed up. Alice was off to Barbados. Simone had been hoping against hope for an invitation from Fliss; in her culture, they didn't celebrate Christmas until 4 January, which meant that she was always kicking around on 25 December. She was absolutely in awe of Fliss's luxuriously vast country house (which Fliss thought very boring and bourgeois), the great big kitchen with the American fridge and the way you could just help yourself to whatever you wanted. No invitation had been forthcoming, however.

Fliss had been totally engrossed in following Ismé about, which threw Simone together with Alice, but they were not a particularly natural pairing and Alice tended to gravitate towards some of the flickier blondes in other forms, leaving Simone once more by herself, a condition she'd been used to in her old school. It didn't seem fair, she thought, that she'd ended up alone again. She'd ignored everything Ash had emailed – she still couldn't bear to see him, not with all the work she had on, plus how embarrassed she was, still, about her size. Ash was tiny, undersized and pin-thin. They'd look like a circus act.

So she remained just old fallback Simone. She buried herself in her books – there were exams the second they came back from Christmas – and withdrew completely. Her teachers couldn't help but speculate: was this guilt? Bitterness? Surely it couldn't be.

Maggie was dreading going home. For most of this term she'd been buried in work and the concerns of the girls. Now she had to face Glasgow again. And everyone would be there, in the same pubs and bars, going to Midnight Mass, hanging out. Was it really only a year since Stan had proposed? She couldn't bear to think about it.

She didn't want to leave school really; she wished she could be like poor Barbie Perrin, whose parents were serving in the military overseas and couldn't take her. She'd be shut up here with Miss Starling and a couple of the other long-haul girls, and however jolly they attempted to make it, it wouldn't feel nice. Not now that everyone else was going home, and there were shouts across the banisters about missing socks, and presents, and whose parents had just arrived and whose mum was looking amazing (the girls were desperately proud of their parents at these events – woe betide anyone who didn't turn up with a new outfit and their roots done).

Simone's heart sank as she saw her father's old estate car pull up next to all the Range Rovers and Jags in the car park. Her brother, who seemed to have grown another five inches in the couple of months she'd been away, slouched out. Astrid Ulverton, who was standing at the window next to her, exclaimed, 'Who's that?' and Simone stared at her, aghast.

Alice didn't care that her parents wouldn't be there; she was hoping to be spotted by someone else anyway. Somebody's mother or father had to be in the theatrical line of work. She rinsed her gorgeous black hair, not noticing Fliss's wistful look.

'I wish I hadn't cut my hair.'

'It's fine,' said Alice shortly. She wasn't really in the mood for reassuring Fliss, surrounded as she was by her loving family and with her new best friend Ismé. 'You'll look perfect for being a little boy anyway.'

Fliss's face began to crumble like she was nine years old, and Alice heaved a sigh.

'Hey,' said Ismé, coming in. Her bag was already packed.

'Are you looking forward to seeing Kizzie?' said Fliss daringly.

Ismé shrugged. 'Hmm,' she said, and Fliss's heart leapt.

'Is she coming?'

'We don't really ... I mean, we don't really stick with cultural insistence on pair norms,' said Ismé, and Fliss nodded as if she knew what this meant, though it sounded like good news. She looked at Ismé, who was made up for her role. Pale frosted shadow on her eyes, right up to the brow line, stark silver eyelashes stuck on, and silver lipstick – stunning, absolutely gorgeous. Fliss wondered for the millionth what it would be like to kiss those strange silver lips, and suddenly found herself bright red with embarrassment.

'You nervous?' said Ismé.

'Yeah,' said Fliss. 'You?'

'I don't care,' said Ismé. There was a silence.

'Come on then,' said Fliss.

Chapter Twenty

Pat had gathered some of the pupils around afterwards to talk about the school. David was feeling on something of a high; it had been a good lesson, and now it was Christmas lunch in the canteen, to be followed in the afternoon by the school carol concert. They didn't do carols as such, but rather Christmas songs that everybody liked, and it was, if not particularly traditional, gigantic fun listening to everyone bellow out 'Last Christmas' and 'All I Want for Christmas Is You'. The kids, almost all of them, were giddy with end-of-termitis, but for once it felt good-natured, rather than threatening, and David was touched by the number of pupils who put their heads round his classroom door to bid him farewell – many of them gleefully waving their mobile phones in his face.

'Yes, yes, yes,' he said, tidying up. 'Read! I don't care if it's the Christmas *Radio Times* – just read *something*, please. Thank you, bye, happy Christmas.'

He didn't even notice that the omnipresent Jazelle wasn't there.

Unfortunately where Jazelle was was in a room with Pat. It had started innocently enough – Pat had asked about the classes she was taking, what she liked and didn't like about the school. And which teachers she liked.

If you have a crush that by necessity ought to be secret, it is extremely hard not to talk about it. And Jazelle could not stop talking about David. It poured out of her: how brilliant he was, how much everyone loved him, how into him she was, how special he made her feel.

Anyone less daft than Pat would have taken all of this with a pinch of salt. Teenage girls, after all. But Pat wasn't letting anything go.

'Do you feel as if he's picked you out?' she asked. Jazelle went bright pink. 'Oh yes,' she said. 'I really feel as if we have a special connection. He spends a lot of time just with me, going through things. We talk all the time. Just us.'

Pat raised an eyebrow. 'Really?'

Jazelle smiled, so happy to be listened to.

'Oh yes. He tells me all the time how wonderful I am. We've been exchanging cards. We really have this connection. He said we should take things further.'

'He said *what*?' asked Pat.

Jazelle coloured.

'Um, yes. I think so.'

'Okay, well, thanks, Jazelle. That's all.'

And Pat trotted off, full of horrified excitement, to speak to Barry Frise. Because, after all, it wasn't like Mr McDonald didn't have form . . .

Chapter Twenty-one

The auditorium was full, thronged with happy parents and happy children. Maggie took her seat at the front. She could see Ismé's mother sitting in the fourth row, next to a girl with long dark hair – the travel grant had come through – and went over to say hello.

'How is she doing?' said Ismé's mother, her gaze shrewd behind thick glasses.

It wasn't an ideal time, but Maggie didn't know when she'd next get to talk to her. She bent down close to the woman.

'She's ... Honestly? I think she could be doing better.'

'I see.'

'She's such a clever girl, so full of talent. But she seems ...'

'Angry?'

Maggie chose her words carefully.

'I'd just want her to be happier. And if you could let us know what more we could be doing, please. To help her with that.'

She paused.

'I want to tell you we're doing everything we can to track down whoever made the racist comments. It's completely and utterly unacceptable and we are not making light of it. We really want Ismé here. We wouldn't like to lose her.'

Ismé's mother nodded.

'Can you tell her that from us?'

Ismé's mum laughed.

'I haven't been able to tell that child anything since she was four years old.'

'Okay,' said Maggie. 'But do you think ... She seems to miss home a lot.'

'Wasn't happy there either,' said Ismé's mum, and Maggie took a little comfort from that.

The girl beside Ismé's mother looked up. She was pretty, but looked very anxious.

'Hello,' said Maggie. 'Are you a friend of Ismé's?'

The girl's lip curled.

'Yeah, whatever,' she said, and went back to being completely engrossed on her phone.

'*Dahling!*' Fliss's mother was making a terrible job of covering up her horror. 'What have ... I mean ... Well.'

'I told you it was dreadful,' said Hattie with a sense of satisfaction.

'Shut up, you cow,' said Fliss, trembling in shame and anger. Their father closed his eyes and wondered again why it was he hadn't had sons to play rugby with, and how much simpler everything would have been.

'Darling, have you been terribly unhappy?' said Fliss's mum, who obviously couldn't imagine any other reason for cutting your hair. Her own was a mid-length bouffant of perfect blonde streaks, expensively done once a fortnight.

'No,' said Fliss, folding her arms.

'Well, I suppose compared to—'

'Compared to what?' demanded Fliss.

'Some of the other stupid things you do for attention,' supplied Hattie, and Fliss shot her a look of pure loathing.

'Ooh, don't diss me, Justin Bieber,' said Hattie.

'Harriet, please,' said her mother, as if her warring children were a mild inconvenience.

There was the ding of the five-minute bell.

'Well, we had better go in,' said Fliss's mother. 'Shouldn't you be backstage?'

'They haven't got a boys' toilet there, though.'

'Shut *up*, Hattie!'

The lights dimmed and there was an expectant hush in the hall. Then white lights came on and suddenly a beautifully painted backdrop of vaguely Dutch roofs appeared as the curtains swung back.

Lovely melancholy music sprang up as Carmen ran on as Gerda, quaint in a bonnet and long apron, but when Fliss appeared in cropped trousers and with that short hair and a butcher's cap, suddenly it all made sense. She was an absolutely perfect Kay – sullen, boyish, utterly beguiling – and her swotting up had obviously paid off; even Alice, waiting grumpily in the wings for her tiny role, couldn't help but admit she was great.

Then the great sleigh was brought on, pulled by ropes, looking magical in the theatre lights, despite the fact that it was made of cardboard and glitter. The little siblings in the audience gasped as Ismé stood up, toweringly beautiful and strange-looking, all in silver and white.

And they gasped even more when, as the queen invited Kay to '*come and kiss me*', Fliss flew towards her and jumped on the sleigh and kissed Ismé full and lingeringly on the lips.

'Oh Lord,' said Fliss's father. 'Here we go again.'

Chapter Twenty-two

David was utterly stunned, still feeling sick. He had had at first no idea who Barry was talking about. Then he'd narrowed it down to one of the girls who came to his extra classes and was often hovering about afterwards. But then suddenly, disastrously, he remembered the card he'd thrown away, and how, of course – of *course* – he should have reported it, and the conversation he'd had with the girl, and how she'd stormed off. How could he have been so stupid?

'Why didn't you tell us about it? For Christ's sake, man,' said Barry, whose disappointment at the idea of losing the school was deep and real.

David could almost hear the mutterings about why he'd had to leave his previous school, and shut his eyes in utter horror. Oh God. How could it all have collapsed so quickly? How was his life just falling into this terrible pit? On the one hand, careers were ruined on the say-so of a child; it did happen, particularly to male teachers – that was why there were so few of them. On the other hand, in the past and even now, teachers had done terrible things to the young people in their care. Everyone knew that.

'Because it was nothing. I'm never alone with a child, it's entirely clear. She's a child, Barry.'

'We'll need to look at these allegations after the holidays. I know her father. He's going to be livid.'

David squeezed his eyes shut. The idea that someone would even consider for second – and from the look in Barry's eyes, he clearly did – that he would touch a child. The very idea. It utterly revolted him. More than most, in fact, because he knew young people well; knew their vulnerabilities, so at odds with the size or bravado they might display to the outside world.

'You know it's crap, though,' he said, his voice quiet.

'I'm not allowed to say anything, mate,' said Barry.

There was a long pause.

'We'll sort this out after Christmas,' said Barry, sagging under the weight of what he was doing.

'Well, am I suspended?' said David.

'I'll have to talk to Jazelle's dad,' said Barry. 'See what's up.'

'See what's up,' said David bitterly. 'That's how it works, is it?'

Barry blinked.

'Look,' he said. 'I know people think I'm not much cop around here. And that things don't work so well. But let me tell you, I'm not an idiot. I know what I'm doing. We'll get this sorted.'

Chapter Twenty-three

Half blind with hurt and misery, David hardly knew where he was driving, through the sharp, frosted night, until he realised with a shock that he had followed a long-familiar road, and that he could see floodlights blazing over Downey Boys. It must be the night of the Christmas show; the girls came over to Downey Boys as they had the proscenium arch, just as the boys trotted over to Downey House to swim in their outdoor salt-water pool (despite their protestations in the earlier months of the year).

He halted and got out of the car. He couldn't help it. The night was clear and still, and the sound travelled. It was the upper girls' choir; he recognised it straight away. They were singing 'Scots Nativity', one of his absolute favourite carols: 'Balloo lammy balloo ballay.' He had never understood the words, but adored the haunting lullaby.

He stood in the frosted grounds as his hands grew cold and red, then realised it absolutely would not do if anyone came across him out here, and reluctantly got back into his car and drove onwards, feeling deeply grave.

Inside the hall, Maggie fingered her necklace. She had always loved this song, and was trying very hard not to cry. She glanced out of the tall windows. In the distance she could see what looked like the lights of a stalled car. But when she looked again, they had gone.

Chapter Twenty-four

Maggie had in fact almost missed the great kissing incident, because Marzia had appeared at the side of the stage, beckoning urgently. She crept away just as Gerda was staring askance at Kay and the sleigh was pulled into the wings.

Marzia was holding up her phone.

'They're at it again,' she said. 'They've just posted.'

Sure enough, there it was

That n*****, it said on the Downey House thread, *doesn't belong in a school like this. Everyone hates her, the stupid show-off. It's pathetic really.*

'When was it posted?' said Maggie breathlessly.

'About twenty minutes ago.'

A huge wave of relief broke through her like ice water.

'But they were all getting changed back then ... all my girls were backstage. I mean, we could see them all. All of them.'

Marzia nodded.

'Which doesn't really help us.'

Maggie peered out from beside the curtains, looking around. It had to be somebody here. It had to be; who else would know when Ismé was onstage?

And then she caught sight of someone. And it all made sense. She felt herself sagging with relief.

'Oh thank God,' she said. 'Thank God. It never even occurred to me.'

'Who?' said Marzia. 'Who are you talking about?'

And Maggie indicated Kizzie, the girl who'd arrived with Ismé's mother, who wasn't watching the action onstage at all, but instead was bowed over, furiously tapping at her phone.

'So what ... some malicious little cow from elsewhere?' said Marzia, bemused.

'No,' said Maggie simply. 'I don't think so. Just someone who misses her friend.'

She looked at Ismé and Fliss waiting for their latest cue backstage, standing defiantly close together.

'Possibly more than a friend,' she corrected herself, as it all fell into place. 'Oh my goodness.'

Chapter Twenty-five

There was juice and mince pies – and mulled wine for the adults – after the performance. Ismé was obviously disconcerted to see Kizzie there, particularly since Fliss was following her about like a lovesick puppy. Alice watched everything, her face hard.

'Hi,' Ismé said coolly as Kizzie tried to throw her arms around her. 'Glad you came.'

'Your mum brought me,' said Kizzie, as if this gave her rights. 'Who the hell is this?' She glared at Fliss. 'Didn't know you were into boys.'

'Don't cause a scene,' said Ismé, which meant of course that the ears of everyone in the vicinity pricked up, in case there was about to be a scene.

'What, in front of your new posh friends? Why not, worried they'll see you for what you really are?'

Ismé was trembling from head to foot.

'And what's that, Kizzie?'

'A two-timing bitch,' said Kizzie.

'Come on, Kizz, don't be such a normie,' said Ismé, stubborn. 'We're not like that.'

Kizzie's face was a mask of misery.

'We were like that! We were! Until you came here so you could run about with these ... prancing show ponies ... '

'Thanks very much,' drawled Alice.

'Shut it,' said Kizzie viciously.

'No, you shut it,' said Ismé surprisingly. She moved closer and snatched Kizzie's phone.

'Hey!'

'Here we are. Catz. Someone's posting. Oh, is it you?'

There was an intake of breath around the room. Everyone had felt, whether they liked Ismé or not, that this was an awful situation. Everyone immediately felt relieved. And much, much happier.

Everyone except Ismé.

'You ... you did this to me?'

'I just wanted you to come back!' wailed Kizzie. 'I just wanted everything to be like it was!'

'By typing this filth about me?'

'I didn't mean it! You know I love you. I just wanted you to come home.'

Ismé, while still in her Snow Queen gown and silver make-up, her long hair tumbling, turned on her heel and, in a move that made pretty much every other girl in the year fall in love with her, dropped Kizzie's phone into the massive vat of mulled wine. Then she swept away and went to find her mother.

'That journey home is going to be awkward,' observed Alice to nobody in particular.

Fliss caught up with Ismé, the talk of the school, just before she left.

'Will you ... can I follow you on Instagram again?' she asked shyly. Ismé reached out and stroked her short hair.

'Sure, sweetie,' she said, and Fliss melted.

'Ismé!' It was Miss Adair.

'I'm so glad it wasn't one of us,' Fliss said quietly.

Ismé, to her surprise, nodded in agreement.

'Me too,' she said.

'Ismé! Your mum needs to leave.'

Fliss kissed her quickly on the lips again.

'Merry Christmas,' she said, alarmed at her own daring.

'Merry Christmas, Kay,' said Ismé, smiling in a tired way.

Chapter Twenty-six

'What are you going to do?' said Dr Deveral after all the performances had ended, the admittedly rather saucy version of *The Snow Queen* having been the undoubted hit of the evening.

'I'm going to speak to Ismé's old school about Kizzie,' said Maggie. 'Just to warn them. It's a terrible thing, that. Terrible. Ismé herself has shown nothing but dignity throughout this entire thing.'

Dr Deveral nodded. 'I'm extremely pleased that this has been cleared up ... well, that bit anyway. Can you talk to the little Prosser girl next term about public displays of affection?'

And now the cars were leaving the car park, wheels crunching slowly through the frost, beams lighting up the high ceiling of Dr Deveral's beautiful office.

'So you're going home for Christmas?' the headmistress enquired.

Maggie shrugged, her good mood slipping.

'Nowhere else to go. I volunteered to stay, but Miss Starling has it covered.'

'Ah yes,' said Dr Deveral drily. 'Miss Starling's poor Christmas mites.'

'Are you going away?'

A small smile played about the headmistress's lips.

'I am . . . taking a short trip as it happens, yes.'

'Ooh, whereabouts?'

'St Petersburg,' said Dr Deveral in a tone that invited no further questions. 'Well, I shall wish you a peaceful time with your family . . . and your fiancé?'

Maggie shook her head, colouring.

'No,' she said. 'No.'

'Ah.'

Both women became uncomfortable with the conversation.

'I'm sorry to hear that.'

Maggie shrugged.

'Well. It is what it is.'

Dr Deveral nodded. She had kept track of David through the grapevine and knew that he and Maggie hadn't been together. The scandal had rippled around for a while and then died down. She congratulated herself on keeping things sensible and nipping it in the bud. But she hated to see one of her best teachers downhearted. Still. Maggie was so young. She had plenty of time for second chances. Whether Veronica herself did was another matter.

'Just you go and have fun,' she said, which was such an unlikely thing to hear from Dr Deveral, Maggie broke into a smile.

'Thank you,' she said. Then she added cheekily, 'You too.'

She would have been very surprised to hear Veronica say to herself after she'd left, 'Oh, I do hope so.'

Chapter Twenty-seven

Oddly, it wasn't quite as bad being home as Maggie had been dreading. It was Christmas, after all, and Cody and Dylan were beside themselves with excitement. The house looked nice all covered in tacky coloured lights; her dad had even put a reindeer on the roof. You couldn't not smile when you saw it flashing on and off.

Term had finished on the twenty-third; it was now Christmas Eve. Maggie had dashed around picking up shopping at the last minute. There wasn't much choice in their tiny Cornish village, whereas Glasgow had everything.

Everyone was going to Midnight Mass, slightly jolly, rather more than slightly tipsy, and Maggie had thought she would just sneak off to bed on her own and have a quiet cry, which was very, very difficult to do when her Auntie Lesley and Uncle Morris had taken her room and she was squeezed onto an air mattress in the downstairs office. Since it wasn't really an office, just part of the sitting room, with double doors between them, it meant she had to wait for everyone else to go to bed anyway, so she decided she might as well go to Mass too. They all giggled and chattered excitedly as they shrugged into their coats, Cody and Dylan shrieking and whacking each other with joy.

She walked down with her sister, who said she was welcome to stay at her flat, but . . .

Anne's flat was neat as a new pin but absolutely tiny. It was privately rented, not council, which meant a lot to Anne, who dreamed of owning her own place one day.

'How's it going?' she said as they stamped through the icy streets, hailing friends and neighbours on their way to the ugly 1970s brick church that stood at the top of their estate.

Maggie shrugged.

'Meh,' she said. They walked on a little further.

'Was it worth it?' said Anne. Maggie turned to her.

'What's that supposed to mean?'

'You know . . . not getting married, all of that . . . '

'You know nothing about it,' said Maggie hotly.

'Okay, okay. I was asking if that fancy school and everything was worth it, that's all.'

'Well, it is,' said Maggie, biting her lip, not wanting to reveal that she had no idea what the answer to the question was.

'Good! Good! No, I'm glad!' insisted Anne.

As they walked on in silence, a very familiar figure stepped out of the shadows. He was staring at the ground.

'Hey,' said Stan.

Maggie lifted her weary eyes. She might as well just get it over with.

'Hey, Stan,' she said. He raised his hand. But it was Anne he was smiling at.

'I didn't think you were coming!' she said happily, and Maggie wondered when they'd discussed their plans.

'Ah, my nan wanted to come, like,' he said, twisting. His grandmother was being helped up the street by a neighbour. She waved to Maggie when she saw her. Maggie didn't know if Stan hadn't told her they'd broken up or if she'd just forgotten, so she waved back cheerily. Anne waved too.

'Ready for the big day?' Anne said, falling into step with Stan. Maggie followed them, perturbed. Was her sister doing this on purpose?

'Aye, well, mostly a quiet one,' said Stan, a fact that was belied by several of his friends coming up and leaping on his back. They stopped short when they saw Maggie there, the confusion evident on their happy red faces.

'Go on in,' said Maggie, thinking she'd wait for her mother, or even just head home altogether. They'd get back later; she might even have managed to go to sleep by then. Okay, so that wasn't very likely. But surely she'd drop off eventually.

She took out her phone to make herself look occupied, and wandered to the side of the church doors as the last stragglers entered and an enthusiastic crowd started up a very loud 'Once in Royal David's City'.

To her total surprise, as she held it, it rang. Midnight on Christmas Eve; it was ridiculous. Who could possibly be calling her?

The number was withheld. It would probably be a computer, one of those bots that dialled phones and tried to sell you central heating. Her finger wavered over the red hang-up button.

Then, hearing the happy chorus inside the church, she found herself prodding accept, just to postpone the moment when she either had to join her family and friends, or crawl back down the hill on her own.

The voice was so quiet it was almost a whisper. But she'd have known it anywhere.

'Maggie? Is that you? It's David.'

SPRING

Chapter One

Maggie clutched the phone and held it away from her face. Was she dreaming? Was it the fact that it was Christmas Eve; how tired she was; how emotional? She stared at the device in her hand.

'Hello?' came the voice.

Maggie glanced around. The bells were still ringing for Christmas; everyone else had gone into the church now. She was alone, her breath in front of her face rising like a cloud.

'David?' She was whispering, although she didn't know why.

There was a long exhalation of breath on the other end of the phone, then silence.

'Uh, hello?'

Now Maggie was starting to feel uncomfortable, her heart beating incredibly quickly. She had no idea at all what he wanted. It could be anything.

The silence grew longer. David screwed up his face; he'd phoned her in desperation, just to hear her voice, but now she was there, he found himself tongue-tied; had no idea what he truly wanted to say.

'Um ... hello,' he said warily.

'Hello?' Maggie said again. David winced. This wasn't helping them move any further forward.

'I just wanted to say ... '

David had the sudden ridiculous feeling that he was about to cry. He thought ruefully of the number of times he'd told the boys in his care that crying was perfectly fine, a natural reaction to the world, and that 'toughening up' was a terrible standard for masculinity. And now, here he was, and he couldn't do it himself. He couldn't say how he really felt, not at all.

'... Merry Christmas,' he finished.

Maggie swallowed hard. It wasn't very merry from where she was standing.

'Oh ... that's nice,' she said. 'Uh. Merry Christmas to you too.'

The silence deepened. Inside the church they'd changed to singing 'The Holly and the Ivy'.

'Well,' said Maggie, angry suddenly that her heart seemed to be ready to break all over again; angry that the sound of his voice had such an effect on her after six months – six months! – had gone by without them being in contact at all. Nothing had changed, and here she was, stuck on an air mattress in the downstairs of her parent's house, aged thirty-one, with damn little to show for it.

'Was nice to talk to you,' she said.

David wanted to kick something. Tell her! Just tell her! Every love poem he'd ever read; all the novels, all the great swooning declarations ... and here he was, on a freezing night, alone, about to let something precious slip between his fingers yet again.

'Maggie,' he said suddenly, boldly. 'Don't. Don't go. Don't hang up.'

'What do you want?' she said wonderingly, and he bit his lip.

'I just wanted ... Oh Maggie.'

Maggie's heart leapt.

'Yes?'

'I ... I've been having ... oh God ... a shit time.'

'Me too,' said Maggie quickly, and there was another pause.

'Oh ... what's up?' said David, like an idiot.

'Um ... just things,' said Maggie, totally unsure where she stood. 'What about you?' she added quickly.

'Oh God. This new school. It's all ... it's just doing my head in, as I think the young people say ... '

'Oh,' said Maggie. She'd thought he meant life was shit without her. Not more school stuff.

There was always school stuff.

'I just thought ... I wanted ... Maybe we could talk about it,' said David, realising as he did so how lame he sounded.

'Maybe you should take it up with your head,' said Maggie stiffly.

'Well, he's involved,' said David, sighing. 'Oh, never mind.'

Maggie couldn't believe how wrong this was going. The only person she wanted to hear from ... calling to complain about his head teacher.

'Okay,' she said, the gulf between them wider than the distance from Scotland to the south-west of England.

There was another silence.

'I ... I just wanted to hear your voice,' said David.

Maggie swallowed hard.

If he'd called and said, please. Please. Let me see you. I miss you so much; to distraction. You are so important to me. I wish we were together.

But she remembered the poem he'd sent her in the summer, the first two lines of which had been enough: *Shake hands, we shall never be friends; all's over. I only vex you the more I try.*

He had been trying ... she didn't know what he'd been trying. He blew hot and cold; he vanished; he didn't speak up; did silly things when it was too late. He behaved like a foolish boy when she wanted a man.

She'd been through so much. She'd lost so much. She needed him to be there for her, and he couldn't be, and she was slowly, gradually learning to accept that.

'It's nice to hear from you,' she said.

But there was nothing. David was in agony, desperately hunting for the words that would make everything all right, but they just weren't there.

'Uh. You too. Happy Christmas,' he said again, hopelessly. He sounded so defeated.

'Are you going to be okay?' she said suddenly.

'Oh me, yes. I'm always okay.'

'Well, good then,' said Maggie, who felt very much not okay. 'I'm glad to hear that.'

She couldn't bear it; couldn't bear that this was going to be it. But as yet another silence fell, she couldn't hang on any longer; couldn't keep living the dream that David was the answer to everything, the answer to her prayers.

'We're not meant to be in touch, are we?' he said hollowly.

Maggie half smiled. It felt so Victorian, the code they'd both had to sign up to.

'No phone calls, no email, no personal contact,' she recited.

'So I could have sent you a Christmas card?' he said.

'Yes,' said Maggie, suddenly angry again. 'You could have.'

'Okay.'

There was one more long pause.

'I have to ask you something,' said David.

Ask it, thought Maggie. Ask me to come over. Ask me to be with you and throw everything to the wind. Ask me if you can love me.

'Did you . . . are you still at the school?'

Everything, Maggie realised, everything was about the poxy fricking school. School school school. Everything was about the pupils and the school and nothing was about her.

'Yes. Yes, I am,' she said.

'Okay then.'

They hung up after that, Maggie upset and hopelessly disappointed that he had fallen so very short; David nervous, furious with himself, but pleased that he had asked the only question that mattered. Are you still at the school? was the surface question; he had assumed she would understand the intrinsic one: did you get married?

And now he knew she had not married Stan, and there was still the tiniest hint of a flame, deep down, the tiniest pinpoint of hope flickering in his breast, even as Maggie went home and drank enough whisky that even her rowdy family returning from church could not wake her.

Chapter Two

Winter stubbornly refused to end, even as the new term started. The daffodils were waiting to bud; the calendar was ticking away towards the warmer months – but nothing.

It was as if there had never been a concept of spring. The idea of being warm, of feeling the sun on your face, had completely faded from Maggie's view; she couldn't even remember what it was like.

Every damn day: tights, socks, vest, shirt, jumper, coat, hat. And that was just to go downstairs to breakfast. The school's policy of not heating the corridors, which parents tended to find so very quaint, had to be reversed simply to stop everyone getting chilblains and whingeing all the time, after Kylie from Sydney and Azura from Barbuda both put in formal complaints.

Snow fell – unusual in Cornwall – and blocked the roads, and there were a couple of frightfully exciting days where the delivery vans couldn't get through and the girls had to head over to the domestic science department (Dr Deveral was well aware that it was called food technology these days, but that had never really caught on) to bake bread, with the other half consigned to outdoor duties, helping the caretaker clear the road and pathways. A merry sight they made, pink-cheeked and laughing, squealing and chattering as they heaved and huffed the snow away.

Snowball fights were, technically speaking, against the rules, but the rules were ignored as the girls charged about the grounds, breathing the biting air and forgetting for a moment the concerns of being a contemporary adolescent: the petty jealousies and deep pashes and all the pressures that being a twenty-first-century girl at an expensive school could bring. The teachers, observing them in their unself-conscious gaiety, couldn't help but reflect how, regardless of kindness of intent, there was always a certain amount of cruelty involved in funnelling a joyous child through ado-lescence and into the long, flat plains of adulthood. Now, though, for once, they could be the children they truly were, and not the adults they were being trained to be.

Maggie just plodded on, bringing in *The Winter's Tale*, and *A Tale of Two Cities*, and Robert Frost and *Morte d'Arthur* and anything else she could think of to suit the short, dark days and the piercing east wind, until the whole of Plantagenet House felt themselves in a deep, mystical trough of snowy woods and frozen lakes and sleigh bells and blazing fires. They were all rather disappointed when the snow finally cleared and cars appeared once more across the fell and normality resumed: a slow trudge towards Easter exams; the last year, for her third-formers, before the exams would mean something very serious indeed.

Maggie was feeling more serious herself these days. She drilled the girls relentlessly; barely noticed anything else around her; refused Claire's offers to take her out for drinks, or Anne's imprecations that she come and spend more time in Glasgow; that everyone was worried about her. This did not help in the slightest.

On one level she knew she was wallowing. On another, she didn't seem to have the will or the energy to get herself out of it. That tremendous jolt she had felt when David had called at Christmas, only to feel so shockingly let down . . . He must, she realised afterwards, just have been feeling lonely. It was basically a booty call and completely inappropriate. And what it told her was that she wasn't ready for healing. Not yet. Not nearly.

At last, on a Sunday morning just before the Easter holidays, Maggie woke in her clean, plain little turret room to something different. Not the low white light that indicated fresh snowfall; nor torrential rain against the windows. Instead, the unusual noise waking her up – annoyingly early, she realised, seeing as it was the weekend – was in fact birdsong. And the frames of gold on her ceiling were sunlight.

It had been so long. The hockey pitch was a mushy mess; the daffodils hadn't even appeared, blown over every time they made the effort. The long months of the beginning of the year had been monotonous and cold. But on the first magical day of spring in Cornwall, it almost felt like it had all been worth it: all the chilly mornings darting out of the shower; all the evenings hovering around the wood-burning stove.

Maggie opened the window and took a deep breath: gorse and wild grass and the salt spray of the sea, all under a sunny sky of brightest Technicolor blue. She stayed there for a while, eyes closed, just taking it all in; feeling her heart open and expand ever so slightly as she inhaled the beautiful scents.

As she padded over to the coffee machine, her first instinct was to throw on some clothes – anything would do – tie back her red hair and just get out of doors.

She poured the coffee into her portable cup and took the stairs quietly – it was too early for the rest of the school to be up – then headed out along the cliff path, her mind, for once, thankfully empty of anything that wasn't glorying in the beauty of the day.

The sea was still bouncy, but it was blue at last, rather than the stormy grey of the preceding weeks and months, and she could already see the little white sails of boats heading out from the harbour, ready to take full advantage of the glorious day.

She found a quiet spot on the headland and settled down with her coffee and the copy of Larkin's collected poems she'd squeezed into her back pocket. The sun was warm enough on her neck for her to barely need the big fisherman's jumper she wore, once she was out of the wind in the comfortable copse. Eventually, leaning back comfortably, she closed her eyes against the sun and, the book falling from her hands, fell into a gentle doze.

She only woke when she felt a shadow fall across her.

For a moment, in her half-awake state, she thought, just for a tiny second, that it was somebody else. That it was David, out walking Stephen Dedalus.

This delicious dream lasted mere seconds, however, as she opened her eyes fully to see Dr Fitzroy looking down on her, smiling in his usual benevolent (and occasionally slightly patronising) fashion.

'Good morning, Miss Adair,' he said. 'Goodness, you haven't been here all night, have you?'

Rubbing her eyes, Maggie sat up.

'Um, no. I don't make a habit of sleeping outdoors, no.' She jumped up and brushed herself down. 'Good morning, Dr Fitzroy.'

'Beautiful morning.'

'Oh yes, yes.'

Maggie looked around.

'It feels like it's been a long time coming.'

'Indeed. Walk with me?'

This was unusual, but Maggie didn't really feel as if she

had any choice, even if he wasn't her boss. Technically. He was still a headmaster and she was still a lowly form mistress.

Over in a far field, she could just make out the white blobs of the new baby lambs, and she couldn't help but smile to see them. They were so comical, bounding up and down with joy, as if they could think of nothing better than their new green world.

'So,' said Dr Fitzroy.

It was something to do with the tone of his voice, but Maggie knew immediately that he was going to talk about David, and she half stiffened and was half immediately interested, because she never got to talk about him for fear of giving herself away; for fear of betraying her old spinsterish reminiscences of something that should be long dead.

'Have you heard from . . . '

'No,' said Maggie immediately. 'We're not in contact.'

' . . . young Mr MacDonald. Ah. I see you're ahead of me.'

Maggie immediately flushed a dark pink, furious with herself for being so obvious.

Dr Fitzroy looked at her curiously.

'You really haven't heard?' he said. 'I thought you young people knew everything about everyone these days.'

Maggie shook her head. David wasn't on any social media at all. At first she'd found this charming. Then infuriating. And now she was glad. She didn't want to think how pathetic she might have been if he had been.

'Well,' said Dr Fitzroy, astonished. And he explained . . .

David had been seriously worried heading into the hearing. The fact was, however much he knew he hadn't done any-thing wrong – and he had examined his conscience quite thoroughly – he realised that he had behaved inappropri-ately; not towards Jazelle specifically, but in the naive way he had failed to realise just how attention-starved some children could be. He had seen it before at Downey Boys, but that was with a child who had lost his father, and he had been well equipped to deal with the delicate emotional situation – the boy was at university now, and doing very well from what David had heard.

This, though, had been a failure to anticipate what was entirely possible in any school but possibly more likely in those with a high level of vulnerable students, as Phillip Dean definitely had. He had been arrogant, he knew; guilty of hoping to coast on his charisma, and when his methods had shown signs of working, he had grown overconfident. He hadn't paid enough attention to the fact that he was paying too much.

And now somebody was going to get hurt.

He carefully put on a sober tie and jacket and sighed. For the first time in his life he wondered if teaching was really for him. It had been such a thrill, finding something he was so good at; realising that he had rapport, could take his love of literature and implant it into growing minds, sharing the joy and enthusiasm he felt for books with children who might be otherwise disinclined to pick one up.

But perhaps he'd be better off as a librarian somewhere. He winced. How could he ever stay quiet?

He tried to damp down his worries about losing another job. Surely people would see that Jazelle's story was just a young girl's fantasies, not anything that had actually happened. But these days, he knew, the rumour mill was so strong and the accusations so febrile . . .

Well, he thought. There was nothing to be done about that but turn up and tell the truth. Dr Fitzroy had kindly been in touch – the school still missed him badly, and the two men spoke often – and offered to write him a character reference.

He had also offered to speak to his previous schools, but David didn't want it spreading more than was strictly necessary.

He felt very alone turning up to the 8.30 meeting at Phillip Dean. A disgraced teacher was indeed a terrible thing, regardless of how merited it was.

As soon as David walked into the room, he realised something was strange. Pat was sitting there already, eating a bacon roll, which seemed odd in itself. She brushed crumbs off her capacious bosom before putting out a rather greasy hand, which David took with some trepidation. Barry was sitting in the corner, looking relieved. And straight ahead was Jazelle, sitting with her father, staring at the floor.

The father's face was crimson with annoyance, his arms folded over his shirt. He glanced up very briefly at David as he walked in but didn't get up.

'Right,' he said.

David looked around, trying to gauge the temperature of the room, but couldn't figure it out.

The father sniffed.

'Do it, Jazelle.'

Jazelle immediately started crying and blinking back tears.

'Take a seat,' said Barry, suddenly realising that he was meant to be in charge of this meeting, and David did so.

There was silence, apart from the occasional wheeze from Jazelle. Despite knowing he absolutely shouldn't respond in any way, David couldn't help asking, 'Are you okay?' in a low voice, which just brought on further sobbing. Pat continued to chomp on her bacon roll, which added a faintly unpleasant aroma to the small, draughty room.

Jazelle's dad nudged her once more.

'Go on then.'

Jazelle tossed her long hair over her shoulder.

'I'm sorry,' she said quietly. David was utterly nonplussed.

'Um, okay,' he said.

'I didn't ... I didn't ...'

She dissolved into fresh hysterics and David started to get rather worried for her.

'Is she all right?' he said to Pat.

'Huh? Oh yeah, girl stuff,' said Pat without looking up.

The father went an even darker pink, which David wouldn't have thought was possible.

'Turns out,' he said, 'she had a bit of a crush on you.'

David didn't know what to do with his face.

'All right,' he said carefully.

'And she was pretending you had a thing going on.'

'I can assure you—'

The father waved his hand.

'Oh, don't worry. Nobody believed it. It just got a bit out of hand, didn't it, Jaz?'

Jazelle sobbed on, her hair completely hiding her face. David wished someone would put an arm round her and comfort her – she was an upset child, for goodness' sake – but obviously he couldn't do it himself.

'These things happen,' he murmured, trying to sound consolatory.

'Yeah,' said Pat, as if her jumping on a teenager's fantasies hadn't given him all this horrible panic about losing his good name and livelihood. She popped the last of her roll into her mouth and chewed loudly.

'Well, all's well that ends well.' And she rubbed her hands on her trouser legs and looked to get up.

'Hang on,' said David. 'Is that it?'

The girl was still sobbing.

'Um, detention?' said Barry warily.

David turned to the father.

'Do you think ... do you think Jazelle could do with maybe seeing someone?'

'Not you,' said the man stiffly.

'*Obviously* not me. I mean a counsellor or something? If she has issues with ... fantasy and so on?'

Pat sighed.

'There's a hell of a waiting list.'

'So?' said David crossly. Then he calmed his tone. 'I'm sure you have enough influence at head office.'

Pat preened.

'Oh, I don't know ...'

David turned to Barry.

'And of course Jazelle can change English classes – it wouldn't be appropriate ...'

Jazelle's dad shook his head.

'Nah,' he said. 'We're taking her out.'

David blinked.

'What do you mean?'

'She's fifteen – sixteen soon. She can get a job.'

David looked at the sobbing teenager. Now that her heavy make-up was practically running off her face, she looked younger than ever.

'She's a very promising student,' he said to her father. 'Perfectly smart. There's nothing to stop her going on to get her A levels, even university.'

The father shrugged.

'Waste of time, innit? She should just get a job.'

'We could look at transfers to a sixth-form college ... What do you think, Jazelle?'

The girl looked up, her face white.

'I think ...' she said. 'I think I'm pregnant.'

The room was utterly silent for a second. Then the father jumped up in consternation.

'By *him*?' he yelled, pointing a finger straight at David.

'Oh for Christ's sake!' said David, who was not by nature given to outbursts.

Jazelle shook her head miserably.

'No,' she said. 'By that bloke in the fifth form who looks like him.'

Everyone had to think about that for a minute.

'Ah, Beanpole Roberts,' said Barry eventually, nodding gravely.

'Who?' said David, insulted.

Pat couldn't help herself from smiling, which was the most aggravating thing anyone in the room could imagine.

'You got yourself pregnant by a boy who looks like the teacher you have a crush on?'

The girl nodded mutely.

David was about to reprimand Pat for the way she was dealing with the vulnerable girl, but Pat had turned to Jazelle and patted her on the arm.

'Oh dear dear dear,' she said, still smiling. 'You *are* in a pickle, aren't you?'

Jazelle shrugged.

'Don't worry,' Pat whispered conspiratorially. 'Worse things happen at sea. And fifteen-year-olds do stupider things every day, I promise. I've seen it all. One does when one is assistant director of school inspections, sub-district Exeter D.' She puffed out her chest. 'We'll get everything sorted, missy.'

The father was still staring at the wall, stunned.

'I'm going to kill that boy.'

'Try not to,' said Pat pertly. 'It really won't help.'

She picked up her folder.

'Okay, Jazelle. We've got a planned pathway for this kind of thing, and the first thing we need to do is sit down with your GP . . .'

David was dumbfounded. He'd truly not really seen the point of Pat before. Even Jazelle had stopped sobbing now that somebody appeared to be offering solutions.

'Well, I feel this has been a very productive meeting,' said Barry astoundingly. He stood up. 'Come along now, everyone.'

David watched the girl trail out as Pat packed up her bag, looking satisfied with herself, and the still shell-shocked dad followed as if he was sleepwalking. Just as he got to the door, he turned back to David.

'Um, sorry about all this.'

'Me too,' said David. He realised suddenly that the two of them must be about the same age.

He watched them leave, wondering about a system where Jazelle's mother couldn't even get a morning off to come to something as important as this, and feeling saddened. But at least she had her family. And possibly even Beanpole Roberts, whom he recalled now. the boy had an almost completely empty head, but a benign and gentle nature. It wasn't entirely impossible that this might work. Stranger things had happened.

Although they did *not* look alike.

And then the room was empty, and there was two minutes before the bell went for morning assembly, and Barry apologetically headed out to smoke a cigarette, leaving David leaning against the door frame, feeling weak with relief.

'Oh God,' said Maggie, once Dr Fitzroy had finished telling her what David had told him. No wonder he'd called her and wanted to talk. He must have felt so alone. Only another teacher could understand how terrifying this kind of thing was.

'I'm not meant to call him or contact him,' she said crossly, kicking her feet as they crossed the fresh green springy moor, forgetting the brightness of the day as she wondered how he was getting on.

'If only there were other ways to communicate,' said Dr Fitzroy gravely. 'Like they did in the old days.'

Maggie looked up at him, but Dr Fitzroy was already taking the path back towards Downey Boys, its old redbrick facade lit up now in the fresh sunlight.

'Tell him to come home,' he said, almost as an afterthought. 'I think he's served his penance. I reckon the board of governors would take him back. The parents are furious he's gone. He isn't listening to me. I imagine he might listen to you.'

Then he turned on his heel and headed back to the school, the boys already spilling out onto the rugby grounds and tennis courts, excited shouts rising as they discovered the newly sprung grass; the world renewed.

Chapter Three

Fliss had adored being snowed in. It gave her time to spend with Ismé, drinking her in. She was mad for her.

Irritatingly, it wasn't remotely clear that Ismé felt the same. She tolerated them hanging out, of course; gave Fliss reading lists of Laurie Penny and Morgan Parker to be getting on with, which resulted in Fliss beginning to sound irritatingly right-on and humourless about everything, which in turn made Alice, who had the peculiarly upper-class way of never caring two figs if she upset anyone and thought being politically correct was tedious and bourgeois, worse if anything, and Fliss would huff and make herself not laugh at one of Alice's particularly cutting insults and therefore was a total drag to be around.

Simone would do her best, but for all her many stalwart qualities, she was not built for jokes, particularly not cruel jokes. Alice desperately needed some distraction and something more fun to do. She missed Fliss as well, missed the adventures they used to get up to.

Now Fliss was madly in love and all moon-eyed and boring and as serious as Ismé when they got up and did their morning yoga together, and it was, it really *was* funny when Simone fell over trying to do the downward dog and squashed her not inconsiderable bosoms, come on, but nobody even cracked a smile and Alice was seriously considering asking for a dorm transfer. Or at the very least planning some mischief, now the sun was finally out.

And now Simone was buried in exams and rushing from place to place and Alice felt very alone.

She played up in class more and more. She still hadn't forgiven Maggie for the Christmas casting – Fleur, after all, would have let her do anything – and she slyly never let her forget, every time they read a poem about lost love, that she knew all about her; never let a chance go by to be late with her homework, or to whisper in a low voice just beyond the reach of being told off. It was never open warfare, but Maggie recognised it as another cross to bear, and it added to her general level of grudgingness and did nobody any good.

Alice also thought about Will, her ex from Downey Boys. He'd wanted to go further than she was ready for – he was sixteen after all; she was only fourteen, and in absolutely no doubt that she wasn't ready to go all the way. And she dreaded looking like Fliss, mooning around after someone who wasn't even necessarily that interested. She'd simply stopped answering his texts, figuring that he'd get the message soon enough, which he did, and that there were always plenty of other girls who'd be interested in meeting up with him, about which she was also a hundred per cent correct.

But the more bored she became, the more she toyed with the idea. She eyed him up in Sunday chapel, when the two choirs mixed together. She hadn't sung in the choir before, and Mrs Offili was (rightly) sceptical when she volunteered. The music mistress had noticed over the years how popular choir became when the boys hit puberty.

Alice's face was so angelic and innocent-looking, though, and she did have a lovely soprano voice – which could be quite something if she ever bothered to work on it, which she didn't, as Alice never worked on anything – so it was hard to deny her.

So while Fliss and Ismé were cuddled up on Ismé's bed, discussing the morality of veganism or blah blah whatever, Alice took to turning up at rehearsals and behaving so well, all her teachers wondered what on earth was up with her.

The weeks when they worshipped at Downey Boys chapel, a beautiful plain grey stone church, much less 'high' than the fussy Victorian building at Downey House, with its ornamental fonts and carved wooden fol-de-rols everywhere, Alice would wear a pretty blue ribbon in her hair, her school skirt just a little too short, but not so much that the teachers could make a fuss about it, as she looked up and down the length of the rugby pitch, choosing her target. Nothing in the first XV, she decided; they all looked like overstuffed monkey suits. Possibly the tennis squad.

But in the end, none of them was as good-looking as Will Hampton, who was singing lustily among the baritones – his band was currently 'on hiatus' after a few rather unpleasant pub open nights where the locals had shown reasonably vividly how keen they were on public school boys putting bands together, i.e. not very. But he did love music.

Unfortunately, and infuriatingly for Alice, he was also dating Carmen Fernandez in the fifth form, a smouldering and totally foxy Spanish girl with a sexy, gravelly voice like Penelope Cruz, a finca in Porto Cervo and a complete and utter lack of interest in third-formers. Will looked smitten, as well he might, and it made Alice furious.

She needed to try a bit harder. Church was really their only chance to meet, both schools being wisely in the business of keeping fifth-form boys and third-form girls as apart as much as was humanly possible.

Alice singing along at the end of the sopranos' row wasn't

going to be enough, she knew, even if she bothered to apply forbidden make-up in the ten seconds before it was time to start, allowing Mrs Offili no time to tell her to wipe it off. Will would join up with his friends after church, laughing and joking, not looking her way, then Carmen possibly would or wouldn't come along – she couldn't even be bothered, which Alice both recognised as how she herself normally felt and was suddenly furiously jealous of – and they would walk back together arm in arm, Alice feeling like the annoying little sister, completely overlooked at the back.

This would *not* do.

Chapter Four

The continuing warm weather felt like a benediction, as Maggie wrestled with how to contact David. Not because of anything; just to say she wished she'd been there for him, not been so taken by surprise and ... well.

On Saturday morning she had driven all the way into Exeter, which had the nearest Paperchase, and spent a very happy hour there – like all book lovers, she had a special affinity with stationery and could happily spend half a day among it – choosing the finest, most beautiful writing paper and pen she could find.

She couldn't help thinking all the time she was there how close he was. How she could easily call him, find out where he was, go round. Oh God. How awful that would be. How awkward.

But a letter. Maybe that would be all right. It hadn't, after all, been expressly forbidden. Social media, email and telephone, no. Handwritten mail ...

As she headed back to the car, she scanned the streets constantly, just in case; even though she knew David hated shopping, was barely sure what it was for. No. Nothing.

She surprised Claire by buying a couple of bottles of nice wine, and the two of them sat out on the tiny terrace of the very highest store room, normally used as storage for the girls' trunks, which was *strictly* out of bounds to students (although the few illicit cigarette ends they found dotted about gave the lie to this). As they drank their wine, Maggie poured out what she was planning.

Claire sighed. She thought Maggie was completely wasting her time on one love affair. Life was about many, didn't she know that? That was what it was to be a happy woman. French women understood this.

'Well, you know,' she said. 'They say love it should be easy, not hard, *tu sais*? That when you find the one you love ... you know. *Immédiatement* it is clear, *voilà*. Until the next time.'

'Really?' said Maggie. 'Well, maybe you go through some ups and downs ... and then it's kind of all right in the end?'

Claire shook her head.

'Bah, *non*!' she said. 'Love ... it is love. When you know, you know. That's all there is to it. As soon as I saw *mon cher* Gerald ...'

Gerald was the thin, bony, aristocratic-looking Classics teacher at Downey Boys, with whom Claire had had a mysterious and dramatic affair that had ended very badly. Maggie had never quite seen it herself, but apparently Gerald's chilly exterior was very much a facade. She also did not enjoy hearing about the intimate sexual exploits of someone she occasionally had to stand next to at all-school assemblies. Claire thought she was lamentably British and bourgeois about this.

Claire fluttered her hands as if further explanations were unnecessary. Maggie got the message.

And she could see it too. When she had met Stan, it hadn't felt difficult. There had been no misunderstandings. They had fallen in love and become part of each other's lives, and that was that.

It had been the unravelling that had been so terribly difficult.

Love shouldn't be ups and downs, misunderstandings. Deep down, if David really loved her, he'd be here. Or she'd be there.

'I barely know him,' she murmured.

'And yet he brings you so much pain,' said Claire, shaking her head. '*Alors.* There are many nice men there for you, Maggie. Many. You should go to Paris. They know how to treat an older woman over there.'

'I'm not an older woman!' said Maggie. She was thirty-one.

Claire waved her hands.

'You know what I mean, yes?'

'No!'

There was a slight *froideur* after that, which Maggie quickly fixed by pouring the rest of the wine into their glasses and changing the subject to their favourite topic: the awfulness of the year head, Miss Starling.

Chapter Five

Mrs Offili knew deep down that Alice wasn't ready, but had decided in the event to let the girl find out for herself what her limitations were. The idea that public school girls were entitled wasn't, she had found, true – many were just normal conflicted children like anywhere else. But you did get the occasional throwback, and Alice was unapologetically that. Mrs Offili rather admired her for it in a funny way. The girls could be so desperate, always worrying about how they looked, or what people thought of them, or how many likes they had on their social posts. Alice genuinely didn't give a damn and, aggravating though it was to try and teach her anything, it was a refreshing take on a world that demanded more of its women than ever before.

Mrs Offili had been born musical; felt music flowing through her veins. She didn't think you found it in girls terrified and throwing up with nerves before major events; practising late into the night. But that was the standard now, even though, with the odd exception – Astrid Ulverton, for example, who basically slept with her clarinet every night and couldn't imagine any other life – none of them were going to become professional musicians. So someone like Alice, who only wanted to do it because she felt like it, and couldn't care less about the consequences, was a breath of fresh air.

'It's a very dificult piece,' said Mrs Offili.

'I don't care,' said Alice, studying the sheet music for Andrew Lloyd Webber's 'Pie Jesu'. 'I'll just give it a shot.'

'That's not really how it works,' said Mrs Offilli. 'You ought to practise a bit with the choir.'

Alice sighed testily. If the music teacher wasn't a hundred and seventy years old (Mrs Offili was actually thirty-eight), she might have a chance of understanding that she wasn't singing to make some special point or to say hi to Jesus. She was singing because Will was coming to church on Sunday and she wanted him to see her. To properly see her.

Alice had never behaved like this for a boy ever and had never thought she would. This was incredibly annoying. She had treated Will quite dreadfully until he'd finally got over her and found someone else, and it was driving Alice to distraction.

It made it worse not to have Fliss to confide in, because Fliss was dizzyingly tied up in her own romantic drama and had basically dumped everyone in her life who wasn't the amazing, perfect, gorgeous Ismé, and Alice didn't really feel like confiding her weakness to anybody else. Still. At least she had a plan.

Chapter Six

Sunday morning dawned, still beautiful, and Maggie awoke with a slightly sore head from the wine and a slightly deeper grump from Claire's words. It was true. If they were going to be together ... well. Why weren't they? It was that simple, wasn't it? She sighed and glanced at her watch, and realised to her supreme annoyance that it was only just past 7 a.m. It was too late to get back to sleep now; she was already wide awake, with things running through her head.

She got up crossly. The beautiful view outside lifted her spirits a little. The green shone like a child's drawing; the lacrosse pitch was perfectly even; the sea was a peerless blue.

There was no one down in the dining room yet, and she helped herself to the Sunday treat of scrambled eggs and smoked salmon on toast, some hot coffee and the papers, before deciding to get outdoors and make the most of the day.

She wandered past the church – Maggie wasn't a believer particularly, but she remained very much a Catholic non-believer, and didn't visit the Church of England more than was required as part of her school day, but it was a pretty sight today, nestled at the bottom of the grounds, next to the verger's little cottage garden, neat rows of carrots just beginning to show. Clusters of girls in their school uniform had gone in; the bell stopped ringing, and there was an attentive silence before the choir started up.

The church was busy; people came from miles around to hear the choir sing – they were a good one and often went on tour in the summer, which was an amazing chance for the children to visit other countries and sing in the great cathedrals of Cologne, Bremen, Reims. They were so lucky. But it did mean you had to turn up every Sunday on the dot, as well as rehearsing twice a week. Mrs Offili wasn't messing about.

Maggie stopped to listen. She smiled to herself at how very English it was: vicars, and old ladies, and green fields. Her old Glasgow friends would find it totally incomprehensible. But she found it rather soothing.

The music finished and there was a hush and a rustle of papers as the vicar welcomed everyone on this fine spring morning. Then the organ started up again, the 'Pie Jesu'. And suddenly there came a voice.

'Piiiieeeeee Jeeeeeeeesuuuuuuuu,' it warbled. But not in a good way. It wobbled and trembled like a drunk Mariah Carey, then abruptly fell off the note.

'Pieeeeee Jeeeessssssssooooooooo.' This attempt was even worse. It was the most ungodly voice.

Maggie couldn't help it. For the first time in a while, a smile crept across her lips. She headed to the open door of the church. There was a high note coming in the next line, she knew, and she didn't want to miss it.

She loitered in the shadows of the nave, eyes struggling to adjust to the light.

'Qui TOOOOOOOOOOllliiissss peccaaaattaaa muuuuundi . . .'
Oh, it was nowhere near.

Everyone was deeply suffering now. Maggie saw Mrs Offili on the organ. She appeared to be playing with her eyes closed. Then she caught sight of the singer.

Rouged to the nines, wearing a very, very short skirt you could mostly see up given that she was standing in the pulpit, was Alice Trebizon-Woods, caterwauling her heart out.

Mrs Offili opened her eyes suddenly and Maggie caught her glance. Hand over mouth, she burst back into the sunlight, where she doubled up and burst out laughing hysterically. All the emotion of the last few months poured out of her, even as she could still hear Alice fervently murdering the song behind her.

'Dona eeeeiiissss reequieEEMMMMMM . . .'

This brought forth a fresh burst of hysterical laughter, just as Miss Starling loomed into view, trying to discover who was making all this noise. Maggie went beet-red trying to hold it in as Miss Starling lectured her on her outrageous behaviour in the house of the Lord. As she swallowed, nodded and staggered away, conscious of the housemistress's eyes upon her, she could hear Alice's final notes – you had to admit, she'd kept at it – winging in the air behind her, bringing on more paroxysms of laughter.

Back at the school, still on a high, she took out the paper she had bought and wrote a short letter to David, addressed to his school, saying she'd heard he'd been through some things and hoped everything was fine now and that he was enjoying the sunshine and please pat Stephen Dedalus for her. Then she put it in the postbox before she could change her mind, completely oblivious of the new Phillip Dean policy that absolutely nothing of an obviously personal nature was permitted to be delivered to any male teacher on the premises; that David would never – could never – receive it.

Meanwhile, outside the church, Will approached Alice directly. Her hair shone in the sun.

'That was brave,' he said to her, smiling his broad grin.

'I know,' said Alice cheerily, giving precisely no shits as to exactly how she'd come across, as long as she'd made an impact.

'Want to go for a walk?'

'Sure!' she said, giving an astonished Mrs Offili the broadest of smiles as they left the church arm in arm.

SUMMER

Chapter One

David had rarely been more buoyed than when he saw Jazelle come back to school for the summer term, even if she scuttled away as soon as she saw him.

She avoided his eye and never stayed late, but he saw her hand in hand with Beanpole Roberts at break time, and once, he even glimpsed her revising in the library, so he couldn't be entirely downhearted about it.

And now exams were upon them.

Normally this time of year for him was highly regimented; filled with rows of silent, cramming students being repeatedly coached to the highest levels to keep up the regular lines of A stars Downey Boys was famous for. Discipline was fierce, but the school also made sure there was plenty of sport, as a physical and emotional release from the pressure, as well as fun days out once the exams were finished. It was an intense, gruelling, worthwhile time, particularly when boys did better than they had expected, while David wasn't bad at comforting the boys who'd done worse.

At Phillip Dean, it wasn't quite the same. Everything was as noisy as usual; there was some chaos involving who was taking their exams where; people were put in for subjects they weren't remotely prepared for and others weren't entered for things they had a good shot at. It was a mess.

David stepped into the breach. He got Liz Garden, the history teacher, onside, taking full advantage – immoral, he knew, but he figured the greater good cancelled out the lesser – of her crush on him to enlist her to help run a study drop-in centre after hours, so he wasn't alone with any of the students. They provided tea, biscuits and vast amounts of moral support from 4 till 6 p.m. every day, and it was astonishing how quickly the group grew from a few desperate students who just needed a quiet space, to more people suddenly realising that actually, passing exams might be something they could do. David dragged in any keen young teacher he could find to do extra catch-up sessions, cajoling the more reluctant pupils who he still reckoned he could get in under the wire.

The Friday sessions normally ended up with the young teachers departing to the pub, and Barry even joined them one evening, fully and firmly astonished at seeing a group of his staff who weren't moaning, crying, leaving or doing all of the above. Instead there was laughter and energy and new ideas and goodwill, and you could feel it in the hallways every day.

And, well, if Miss Garden did flirt and sidle close to him and insist on staying and being last in the pub with him . . . She was pretty, thought David vaguely. It wouldn't necessarily be the worst thing. She was petite and snub-nosed and had nice shiny hair and laughed a lot (he didn't realise that this was part of a plan) in a nervous kind of way, which was very endearing in its own right, and one night when they were ready to leave, he accompanied her outside and gallantly found her a taxi, and she looked straight at him and said, 'Want to hop in?' and he found himself very tempted indeed and remembered the old rules didn't apply here, but even so, he smiled ruefully and said, 'Best not, eh? School and everything,' and she nodded, thinking he was being held back by professional courtesy and deciding to find a new job as soon as she could then call him up again.

(She did, in fact, apply for a much more senior job at a much more senior school, got it, loved it and found her ex was working there and in fact he wasn't nearly as annoying as she remembered him, and a head of department now, and they ended up getting married and living happily ever after, so don't worry too much about Miss Garden.)

He was feeling thoughtful that evening, though, wondering why what was so easy for other people – a young woman, a beautiful night, an open cab door, a ready laugh, a clear invitation – was so difficult for him. What was he holding onto, after all? Just a fading dream that made him wince to remember it.

He stuck his hand in Stephen Dedalus's fur as they turned down the little road where he lived, and got back to the house, still lost in thought.

On the computer was an email from Dr Fitzroy. Trying to get him to come back again, he thought. He half smiled. It was a shame Dr Fitzroy didn't know that he was doing . . . well, he wouldn't say 'brilliantly'. But he'd certainly known it worse.

He looked at the subject matter, shocked for a second, then sat down and read it again, then again.

Little Ash.

Oh no.

Ash was one of their more difficult characters. A scholarship boy, absolutely brilliant, undersized, incredibly chippy, without a mother but with an overbearing and pushy father who tended to turn up at the school dressed always slightly wrongly – shiny suit, wide tie – and be rude and blowhard to staff as if that was how he thought he was meant to behave, boasting endlessly about Ash's genius as the boy blushed hard and stared at the ground as if he wanted it to swallow him up.

A suicide attempt. The most terrifying, the most dreadful words a teacher could ever hear. That a young person in their care could have done something ... could feel things were so hopeless ...

David stood up. He would get some sleep, then head right over. He had been the boy's form tutor, and remembered him with great fondness. And if Dr Fitzroy thought he should be there ...

He glanced at his watch. Midnight. He'd be fit to drive again in, what, four hours? He should try and get some sleep.

He got absolutely no sleep. He wished, in fact, that he'd gone home with Liz Garden. Then he wouldn't have got the news until later and ... well.

He was so lonely. So very, very lonely, it occurred to him, getting bad news in the middle of the night and having nobody to share it with. His father would be asleep by this time; his brother was still out in Afghanistan. It was just him. And that was terrible in its own way. How alone Ash must have felt, to do this.

As soon as he legally could, he took to the car. The roads were silent at that time of the morning, and the breaking dawn was suggesting another beautiful day as he tore up the dual carriageway. He remembered so vividly the day Ash had arrived. The father had been talking about tipping the masters, of all things. It had been utterly awful. And Ash had known it was awful; had cringed and shaken.

The boys weren't bad lads on the whole at Downey; the

ethos was never really to leave them enough free time to get into bullying and to make sure they were too exhausted by the end of the day to try.

But of course it did exist. And Ash was just one of those kids who had it written all over him. Small, loud and under-sized – odd, given the girth of his father – and with the habitual nervousness of children who had lost a parent, his very stance seemed to invite people to rag on him.

David rarely got angry, but when he'd caught Espenson – who was a huge rugby-playing star and had absolutely no need, in David's opinion, to get his kicks out of being malicious to a smaller child – he had given him a roaring dressing-down Espenson had never forgotten.

Even so, Ash rarely had a friend; he was always the fourth in dorms rather than finding a gang of his own; tolerated rather than liked, even as his awful father swaggered up and down every end-of-term pretending they were off on expensive holidays when it was acutely obvious to everyone that they weren't.

The odd thing was, it wasn't snobbery. Plenty of scholar-ship boys got on totally fine with everyone and didn't care; in fact, many gained kudos for being a little bit 'street' in a way the more traditional Downey Boys attendee could simply never claim.

But not Ash. He had an exceptional ability in mathematics, but he wasn't remotely sporty, didn't play an instrument, didn't enjoy drama or film club. Even the nerds left him alone, which was profoundly and deeply unusual. David had always watched out for him and found him rather a heartbreaking child. But this . . .

When he got to the school, the sun was fully up and there was the cheerful smell of bacon frying and the familiar shouts of the boys getting ready for rugby that morning and the general cheerfulness you will hear anywhere when a group of people have woken up on a Saturday morning and the sun is shining.

David felt a quick, sudden tug of homesickness. Things were going well at Phillip Dean, he supposed. But this . . . the muddy boots, the cheery yells, the thwacking of the cricket team out and warming up already – *his* cricket team, as he'd always thought of it.

Well. This was home.

Dr Fitzroy saw his face.

'Ah, knew you'd come back to us sooner or later,' he said, nodding. 'I'm so sorry it took this to do it.'

'How's he doing?'

Dr Fitzroy's face darkened.

'Ah, a bad business,' he said. David nodded.

'I know.'

'He asked for you.'

'I'm sorry,' said David. This was one of the heartbreaks of any teacher's life. You could be proud of the successes. But you couldn't keep hold of the failures. He swallowed hard as they walked together to the san.

'Where's his father?'

'On his way,' said Dr Fitzroy. 'I'm *slightly* worried he'll make things worse.'

David nodded as the headmaster knocked gently on the door. Matron was looking concerned.

'It's . . . I mean it's superficial, the wounds,' she said. 'But he's going to need a lot more . . . they're probably going to want to admit him. Psych is on its way.'

Dr Fitzroy and David exchanged glances. The CAMHS provision in the county was pitiful, absolutely pitiful. Other parents could whisk troubled children off to expensive support facilities. But Ash's father had no such option. There had been stories of children locked up on adult wards; all kinds of awfulness. It was a very grim thought.

The boy looked pale and tiny in the bed; incredibly small for a third year. His face lit up briefly when he saw David, though.

'Mr McDonald!'

'Hello,' said David, smiling kindly. He sat down beside the boy. 'What mess have you got yourself into now, then?'

Ash's face began to wobble a bit.

'Don't be cross with me,' he said quietly.

'I'm not remotely cross,' said David. 'I'm worried.'

'Well, don't be worried neither.'

David looked at the bandages wrapped around the skinny wrists.

'Oh Ash, for heaven's sake. Just tell me. What happened?'

Ash immediately burst into tears.

'My girlfriend dumped me!' he wailed.

David and Dr Fitzroy exchanged glances. Well, this was unexpected.

'Um,' said David. 'Oh no, that's terrible.'

Actually – and considering the cuts the boy had made were superficial cries for attention rather than deep wounds – there was probably something relieving about the fact that there was an explanation, rather than a sinister deep depression at work. It wasn't ideal. But it wasn't unheard of for teenagers in love to go overboard.

'Is she ... at Downey?' asked Dr Fitzroy carefully. Ash nodded.

'It's Simone Pribetich,' he said, bursting into fresh floods of tears. 'I just love her so much.'

David started.

'I know Simone,' he said. She was one of Maggie's

troublesome class. Although he didn't think Simone herself was the least bit troublesome.

Dr Fitzroy blinked.

'I'm not sure I know which one ...'

'Can I see her?' said Ash. 'Please?'

'I'm not sure that's the best idea at the moment,' said David. 'Your father is going to come, and then we're going to have the doctor in to decide on the best thing to do for you.'

'The best thing to do for me,' said Ash, 'is to let me see my girlfriend. My ex-girlfriend.' And he burst into tears again.

'Keep this news from the girls' school at all costs,' ordered Dr Fitzroy. 'The last thing we need is a dose of hysterics on our hands.'

Chapter Two

'Oh my Gawd! Oh my Gawd!'

Maggie had been trying to have a quiet breakfast and read the papers, and suddenly gathering around were large clumps of girls weeping and clutching each other. Oh no, surely not another DJ had died.

'What ees thees?' Claire hissed, sitting next to her, angrily ripping at a croissant as she did every Saturday, as if it wouldn't be easier to just not have one.

'Celebrity death,' predicted Maggie. 'Probably someone you've never heard of. They get themselves in a right state.'

But she was wrong. A sobbing Fliss wobbled up to her.

'Miss! It's Ash!'

Maggie had to search her brains for a second before remembering. That tiny little boy Simone had spent time with last year, 'spent time with' a euphemism for 'snogged the face off on the school bus'.

'Oh my God,' she said, jumping up. 'Where's Simone? What happened?'

But there was absolutely no getting any sense out of the girls, who had differing opinions as to whether he'd thrown himself off the bell tower, hanged himself in the assembly hall or any variety of dreadfully grisly ends. With trembling hands, Maggie pulled out her phone to call Dr Fitzroy.

'Ah, hello, Maggie,' he boomed in his usual genial manner. 'I've just spoken to Matron – physically it's nothing to worry about.'

'Oh my God, is he all right?'

David's head had suddenly jerked up like a meerkat and he was finding it hard to breathe.

'Yes, yes, just a bit of a commotion, you know. We were trying to keep it away from our fair and delicate sisters.'

David and Maggie winced in tandem. Maggie bristled at the way Dr Fitzroy talked about the girls' school sometimes, though the headmaster never noticed and wouldn't have cared if he had.

'And he's okay?'

'Just a cry for attention.'

'Well, he'd better get some then,' said Maggie. 'Wait, hang on . . .'

From the other end of the line David heard a crash and hysterical sobbing.

'I need to see him! I need to see Aaassshhhhhhhhhh!'

Dr Fitzroy sniffed.

'Is that the young lady in question?'

'Pleeeeeaaaase!'

'Simone,' said Maggie quite sharply. 'Calm down. Please. Would you mind stepping away for two seconds and I'll see.'

Simone burst into ever louder sobs.

'It's my fault! Because I've been working too hard. And because of my *breaaasssssts*.'

'Oh God,' said Maggie.

'Bring her over,' said Dr Fitzroy. 'We'll talk to the psychiatrist and see what they say.'

Maggie wondered if the psychiatrist might have time to see both of them.

Chapter Three

In the event, the psychiatrist decided, given the enormous amount of wailing coming from both sides, that treatment was needed but could probably wait a little while. Maggie got the news on her phone walking Simone over.

Actually it was good for Simone to be separated from everyone else sobbing, and Maggie put her arm around her as they walked the mile over to the boys' school under the warm sky.

'Simone,' she said urgently. 'This is emotional blackmail, you know. You mustn't ever give in to it. If a man threatens to do this . . . he's not safe to be around.'

Simone shook her head.

'It's my fault,' she said.

'Oh, I promise you it isn't,' said Maggie. 'Never think that. I mean it, Simone.'

'We were in love,' said Simone. 'And I . . . I let him go.'

Maggie gave her a stern look. 'Talk me through it.'

Simone shrugged.

'Well. You know. Exams.'

'And you didn't want to date him any more?'

'I did!' said Simone with a fresh burst of crying. 'But I've got all of these exams.'

Maggie straightened up.

'But I thought you were taking your exams early because they were so easy for you! I thought it was just to get them out of the way.'

'Nothing is easy for me,' Simone said quietly.

Maggie blinked. She had genuinely thought Simone's exceptional standard of work was natural talent.

'Well, do them next year then.'

Simone shook her head.

'My mum's told everyone. And anyway, I've done all the work now.'

Maggie sighed.

'Oh Simone. I feel so stupid I didn't notice you were under so much pressure.'

Simone shrugged.

'You had things going on,' she said shyly, casting her eyes to the side and glancing up, wary of talking in such an adult way to a teacher.

'Yes, well, that's enough,' said Maggie, and was so deep in thought she almost didn't notice David in the room until she was standing right in front of him.

Chapter Four

'Oh!' said Maggie simply.

They stood, staring at each other. Her face went absolutely bright red and she found herself unable to remember why she was there.

David had had a few more minutes to get used to the idea and had tried to arrange his face and hair and shirt into a slightly more relaxed combination, but it wasn't working out very well for him. Instead he was jiggling up and down on his toes and bouncing about. Dr Fitzroy had a private smile on his face watching them both.

'Um,' said David, his voice slightly squeaky. 'Hi ... hello, Miss Adair.'

Maggie swallowed hard.

'Mr McDonald.'

He looked thin, she noticed. Well, he'd always been thin; tall and rangy, but ... His hair was longer, too, flopping over his forehead, in need of a cut. She liked it. He was wearing a clean, faded shirt that looked like it was about ninety years old.

She smiled at him anxiously, cautiously, and in return got a very quick flash of that slightly manic grin that could take over his whole face before his serious look reasserted itself.

'Can I see Ash?' said Simone, tear-stained and unable to concentrate on anything else.

'Five minutes only,' said the psychiatrist. 'Then we're going to have to talk to him, all right?'

'Are you going to take him away?'

'Five minutes,' said the doctor, ignoring her.

Inside the small sanatorium, Ash looked absolutely tiny and very pale on the bed.

'Ash!' Simone launched herself at him, a large presence on the bed, engulfing him.

'Simone!'

She smothered him with hugs and kisses.

'Look at your amazing bosoms!' said Ash, not sounding remotely suicidal.

'Oi,' said David. 'None of that, please,' and Maggie, flaming, stared at the floor. She couldn't look at him. It was like looking at the sun. Simone moved slightly so she was sitting on the edge of the bed and the pair started talking furiously, and the two teachers moved to the back of the room.

'So . . . ' began David timidly. Maggie stared down at her hands. They were trembling. 'How have you . . . '

There was a crash at the door and the loud voice of Ash's father could be heard in the corridor.

'Simone,' said Maggie urgently. 'Come away.'

She took the girl by the arm, gently, and guided her away just as the tall, red-faced man appeared, suddenly lost for words as he saw his son in the bed.

David was anxious. He was worried about this insecure, bombastic man; concerned that he would channel his fear and upset into anger at the boy.

He needn't have worried. The big man dropped to his knees, grabbed Ash's wrists in his hands and buried his huge head in the boy's chest.

'Ashok,' he said, sobbing. 'Ashok! What have you done? What have you done?'

For the first time, the boy sounded worried.

'Nothing much,' he said. 'Seriously, Dad, don't worry. It's not that bad.'

'You tried to kill yourself,' said his dad. 'Oh my God. My son. This life ... the only life you have ... this happens all the time, you know! Something that you would have forgotten in a week or a month ...'

Quietly and imperceptibly a woman had entered, carrying a clipboard. David correctly assumed she must be the other psychiatrist. She was listening attentively, waiting for the right moment to introduce herself, and she and David smiled at each other rather awkwardly

'This happens all the time to teenagers!' said Ash's father. 'You mustn't do it! You mustn't! Everything will get better! It is so stupid, so stupid!'

'No!' said Ash, sitting up. 'Look!'

And he unravelled the bandages around his wrists. His father looked at him for a second.

'What ...'

The two cuts, one on each wrist, were almost imperceptible; basically scratches. The big man frowned. Ash lowered his voice.

'It was a cry for attention.'

'From me? But you know, Ashok, I am working shifts, I can't move to—'

Ash shook his head.

'Not you! That girl! Did you see her?'

The man frowned.

'The girl ... who was just here?'

'Isn't she awesome?' said Ash proudly. 'She'd dumped me for some stupid exams. So I thought I would show her.'

Ash's father straightened up, then turned round as if noticing the psychiatrist for the first time. He approached her.

'Can you fix my crazy son, please? And tell him to stop scaring his father, who loves him for no reason?'

The woman smiled tightly. 'Crazy's not a word we use, sir.'

'Did you not hear what he just said?'

'I'm not crazy,' said Ash cheerfully from the bed. 'I'm in love!'

Chapter Five

David caught up with Maggie and Simone dawdling on the lawn outside, waiting for news, while being eyed up by various groups of boys. There was a twitch to his mouth as he hurried towards him. Maggie was struck suddenly by a wave of familiar emotion as he moved quickly – David never moved slowly – beneath the avenue of blossoming trees that led to the entrance of the old grey school.

'Well?' she said. 'How is he?'

'Simone, could you leave us for a moment?' said David.

'Is he going to diiiieee?' wailed Simone.

David blinked.

'Oh. No. No. Definitely not,' he said.

'I love him soooo much!'

'Well, I think he's going to be very glad of that.'

'Can I go back in?'

David shrugged. 'Yes, I should think so. Soon, anyway.'

Simone scampered off back to the san, and Maggie and David were left looking at one another. The spring blossom drifted down on them like confetti at a wedding.

'He's really okay?'

'I've had worse shaving cuts,' said David, smiling.

'Oh, thank God,' said Maggie, shaking her head.

'Well, thanks very much. They were actually very sore shaving cuts.'

Maggie grinned.

'Daft boy.'

'Psychologically ...' David glanced at the retreating form of Simone, 'he may also be fine, yes.'

Maggie clutched her hand to her front.

'I got such a fright.'

David wanted to tell her to come to him, to come and lay her head on his chest, let him soothe her. But suddenly he found himself surrounded, mobbed by boys delighted to see him, asking if he was back, if he was back for good, if Ash was okay, if he could come and coach the cricket team again, please, sir, the new teacher didn't get it, sir, did you come to see Miss Adair, sir? Wooo, sir!

David calmed them all down and looked at Maggie, standing smiling at him with the blossom tossing behind her. Her face was a picture of anxious regret, mixed with the tiniest amount of hope.

'I have to get back,' said David to massed boos from the boys. 'I don't work here. Not any more ...'

Maggie nodded to herself quietly.

'I'll need to get Simone back too,' she said.

'Of course,' said David.

They stood there for a moment. Then she turned to go.

Oh sod it, he thought. He didn't work here. He could do what he wanted.

He made to go after her. But he was still surrounded by boys. It would get back to the girls' school in no time. He'd risk Maggie's job. It didn't matter if he worked here or not, after all the scandal. He couldn't do that to her.

'See you then,' he said weakly, as Simone, beaming and in love, re-emerged, and the two of them walked away.

Chapter Six

There had been a very sober assembly that afternoon, hastily called, in which Dr Deveral had talked them all through the hysteria of suicide, how devastating and infectious it could be, which Maggie, deep down, wasn't sure was as helpful as just ignoring it. But then she was lucky – they'd never had one. Some schools that had experienced it had been blown apart; the child's life, their friends, their families, the community, everything lost in that ultimate act of horrific violence.

'Cries for help will be dealt with, but please, please cry before it gets that far,' said Dr Deveral. 'We're all here. We're all listening. Come to us; come to Matron or your form teacher. We are all here to listen to any worries or niggles you have, no matter how small. Please. Never, ever let it get this far. We can help, and we will. We're your school. We're your home. And I never, ever want a single pupil of mine to feel ignored.'

Maggie didn't know what to do afterwards, trying to get it into Claire's brain for the nth time that suicide wasn't a verb in English and that nobody had suicided, and went to drive into town to clear her head a bit.

Oh, what a day. What a stupid, difficult, terrible day. She had wondered for so long what it would be like; what it would be like if she saw him again.

And looking at him standing there, as handsome as ever, she had realised that the longing was just as strong. Oh for goodness' sake. What was it going to take? What was going to do it? She didn't even know where she was headed; just that she had to get away somehow.

There was a piece of paper entangled in her windscreen wipers, which was unusual. Usually the groundskeepers were thorough, and the girls knew on pain of death not to drop litter. She picked it up and unrolled it.

She recognised the handwriting immediately and her heart nearly stopped. That beautiful cursive, legacy of one of the very few grown-ups left on earth who actually spent their time writing with a fountain pen.

She glanced up, but there was nobody around, nobody who might be looking at her as, cheeks pink, hand shaking, she started to read.

It was a very simple note. For once. There were no grand gestures. No ridiculous train stopping, or declarations of taking her away to Italy, or running along platforms.

No fancy poetry. No losing jobs; no fiancées. No embellished fancy words. Nothing but himself, on the paper.

One word. Just one, very simple word, written down very simply – 'please' – printed on the back of a flyer for a new café in town Maggie had never heard of; that David had taken, unthinkingly, when a nice young chap had handed him one earlier.

Maggie googled the restaurant and plugged it in, then did it again, because the first four times she'd got it wrong as her hands were shaking so much, or she didn't believe it, or she was terrified she was getting it wrong and couldn't bear – couldn't *bear* – the idea of going to the wrong place, which made her even more sweaty-palmed and worse at getting the address typed in on the stupid, *stupid* tiny buttons on her phone, and it offered a route, and. Well. She had to take it.

In the car. Why didn't she keep make up in the car? She rooted around her handbag, and pulled down the little mirror to look at her reflection. Oh God. Seriously. She'd looked like that all day? Seriously. That's how he'd seen her. She took a deep breath and tried to relax. Think something positive, even as she was so desperate to get moving. The sun had brought her freckles out, she noticed. Did she have time to go and change?

Her hands were shaking so much. And it suddenly struck her: when had he left the note? It could have been hours ago; assembly had taken ages! Maybe he'd stayed, then thought she wasn't coming, then gone again. Why had she hung around chatting to Claire?

Suddenly, she was absolutely convinced that he was gone. That he'd been there; he waited; she hadn't shown up, and he'd decided that was that, and moved on. This was – it had to be, after this – her last chance. Their last chance.

At that horrifying thought, she put on the last of her lipstick, blotted it badly with a very old tissue, tried to get her hands through her hair, failed, then also failed to start her little car without stalling it four times.

Calm down, calm down, she told herself. Just calm down.

It didn't work.

Chapter Seven

Obviously the idea that being associated with a suicide bid would make you incredibly popular and an object of fascination was a terrible and wicked thing.

Nonetheless, that was more or less what happened to Simone. She wasn't used to having so many eyes on her, and went very pink as she crossed the hall after the special assembly and mounted the staircase with trepidation

The other girls were in the dorm already, technically doing prep but actually gossiping their faces off. Alice was torn between wanting to tell all about her Will triumph and wanting to hold off, given that Simone was obviously the story of the day.

'It's romantic, though,' Fliss was saying, trying to touch Ismé's hair.

'It's rich, privileged and selfish,' said Ismé while Alice snorted.

'Ash is literally the least rich person in this entire postcode, and I'm including the gardeners and the tramp who sleeps down the bottom of Heartscote Lane.'

'Did you mean dispossessed person?' said Ismé snottily.

'No,' said Alice. 'I meant tramp.'

Simone sidled in.

'Simone!'

They all jumped up to give her a hug.

'Are you okay?'

'I'm really sorry,' said Fliss. 'I didn't know he was going through this.'

'Me neither,' said Simone. 'I just thought it would be better for both of us ...'

'Don't go back to him because of this!' said Ismé in a warning voice.

'Well, duh,' said Alice. 'Thanks for your wokeness in pointing that out.'

'Stop it, you two,' said Simone. 'I'm not going back to him because of this. He'll have to go home for a bit anyway. Just while they check out how crazy he is.' She smiled. 'Mr McDonald said he barely scratched himself.'

'Thank God,' said Alice.

'Mr McDonald's here?' said Fliss, going pink. Alice looked at her.

'I thought you liked girls now,' she said.

'Love isn't binary,' said Fliss, going pinker still. 'Is he still here?'

'No, he left.'

'Did Miss Adair see him?' said Alice. 'Ooh, what was it like? Electricity shooting through their fingertips?'

'They didn't really speak to each other,' said Simone, shrugging.

'Oh, that's a shame,' said Fliss.

'Don't be daft,' said Alice. 'That means they're still mad about each other. If they didn't care, they'd be chatting.'

Fliss looked at Ismé, who shrugged. 'I agree with Alice,' she said.

'Ooh,' said Fliss. Ismé and Alice smiled at one another.

Chapter Eight

This was the part of teaching they never let you see, thought Dr Deveral, slumping back in her office chair.

The horror, the sheer terror and horror of losing a child – and not to an illness, or a tragic accident, dreadful as those things would be, but to their own hand, because they were so very miserable. It didn't bear contemplating.

Robert Fitzroy had spoken to her, reassured her it was absolutely nothing, the smallest of cries for attention and in fact the psychiatrist had evaluated Ash as not benefiting remotely from in-patient treatment – he would be seen three times a week to, as she had termed it, 'reorientate appropriate response levels'. The father was tearful with relief; the child even appeared to have his girlfriend back, which was not ideal, they agreed. Still. It had not been serious. Even so, they would now have to haul out every single child in the school and make sure they weren't secretly miserable, which was a manpower problem however you looked at it.

Dr Deveral felt absolutely teary, mostly with relief. She didn't normally let the ups and downs of the children get to her, otherwise she'd be an emotional basket case. But today ... There was something about Simone, that dear, stodgy, serious girl, inspiring such great heights of passion.

As Miss Prothergill brought her her customary cup of

tea, she saw Dr Deveral's typically severe face soften, very briefly, into something that looked like a tiny laugh, immediately stifled.

To hide it, Veronica clicked her email and to her surprise saw a message she wasn't expecting. Hadn't been expecting at all.

And the opening characters were in Cyrillic . . .

Chapter Nine

The place on the flyer was called Reuben's. It was a new, funky, hipster bar – not necessarily at all what David would have chosen, but actually rather nice – exposed brick walls, rough wooden tables, good coffee, large jugs of cocktails, healthy young people everywhere having a nice time. It had apparently been opened by a rich local American who wanted to help unemployed youths in the area, and he made a mental note to send some of his Phillip Dean students down there. Plus almost all the cocktails appeared to contain copious amounts of local honey, which was curious.

It was still a glorious evening. There was no sign of Maggie. He wondered ... oh God. Had she got the note? Maybe it had blown away. Maybe she hadn't – the thought struck him, and suddenly became absolutely exactly what had happened and he wanted to run back ...

And then he told himself, no. No. No more. He couldn't stop chasing something that just wasn't there. He was going to sit out, on a beautiful evening, and breathe, and deal with it, and the future.

So, trying to calm himself, David ordered the whisky honey special and took one of the pretty old seats outside on the terrace, where there was a good view of the sea and happy-looking surfers catching one more wave, and took out his book – an old edition of *A Tale of Two Cities*, which he had been reading with his fifth-year class at Phillip Dean.

And that was how Maggie found him, half an hour later, having barely moved, so engrossed in his book that she wondered if he'd forgotten she was coming; his long legs folded one on top of the other, his drink barely touched, the pink of the setting sun glowing lightly on his unruly hair as groups of young people laughed and flirted and joked all around his oblivious form.

She stood still, staring at him, her breathing fast, her face burning. She tried to calm herself down; to be cool and collected when he saw her, as if she was a casual, elegant woman of the world, like Claire, unaffected, an independent character who didn't need him, who wasn't desperate about him.

But looking at him, she realised finally: this was it for her. She loved him. She wanted him. This was all she wanted.

She thought of her job. Exam season was going to be upon them soon; the rush and the worry of it; the beautiful days; the lovely long-limbed relief of the girls, laughing and free, as they finished, many of them, thanks to the good ministrations of the school, ready and prepared for a summer of fun and freedom before whatever came next in their gilded lives. It was hard not to envy them, really; hard also not to be proud of what they'd achieved, proud of her own hard work too.

Could she give all of that up for this strange, mercurial man? She might never get another job. Her reputation might follow her everywhere. Or assuming she did, could she leave behind the school she had learned to love so much? Could she give it all away? She'd already left behind a mess in Glasgow; could she do it?

Then he looked up and saw she was there, and his face split into such a beautiful smile, it completely took her breath away. And then she knew, beyond a doubt.

He discarded his book; his hands, he realised, were trembling.

He stopped for a moment, just staring at her as the setting sun caught her flaming hair, then, finally, decisively, all doubt behind him, with everything settled, he stood up and slowly and confidently, walked towards her, and said her name.

Chapter Ten

Now. This is a book which concerns schools, and schoolgirls. It is not inconceivable that it might stray into the hands of a younger person. Therefore a certain amount of decorum is required.

Nonetheless, one might surmise – as Maggie herself had, when she was desperately trying to pretend that she wasn't in love with David over the preceding two years – that a man who reads a lot of poetry and cares a lot about books might therefore be something of a wimp; a shy, nerdy type when it came to sex.

And one might then find that they had been, in fact, totally and utterly wrong on this point: that a man who reads widely, who likes the world enough to explore it constantly; who genuinely adores women and has read a lot about what they think and what they like has, in fact, quite the advantage.

And one might also note that there is a difference between thin, and lithe and strong, and remark upon David's expression of highly serious intent, his joking nature flipping in an instant to something which required all of his studied attention.

If we were going to go there of course.

If we were going to go there we might mention too,

Maggie's embarrassment at taking off her clothes in daylight; the realisation that nobody had seen her naked since Stan, and she wasn't thinking about Stan.

We might note that David, courteously, but gravely, asked for permission, and Maggie, who would, in normal life, had she been giving advice to a girlfriend would have recommended slowing things down, taking things at their own pace, not throwing all her eggs in one basket and so on and so forth, found, immediately, that none of that mattered a whit and said, I will, and shook her hair down the back of her neck as David made a sharp intake of breath.

So, then perhaps you would say he had stood behind her and very carefully and slowly pulled down the strap of her bra and kissed the mark it had left on her pale skin and Maggie had closed her eyes in a ridiculous mix of excitement and relief and disbelief and for a moment they were both completely stock still in the pale washed room, both of them, and the hubbub below the window ceased, and all she could hear was his tortured breathing, and the lightest touch of his hand on her shoulder set her on fire, and the next thing she knew, they were both hard slamming against the wall, struggling to breathe, her entire body on fire, all shame forgotten as she was absolutely desperate to feel every inch of him pressed up against her.

And you may have caught, a little later, if you were passing, just faintly, on the breeze above the noisy and cheerful beach bar, that single sharp, surprised intake of breath; a gasp that turned into a wail; a steadily building heat; a pale white sheet flapping from a bed; a sea breeze cooling a torrent of sweat all the way down Maggie's spine.

And noted that one person swore, violently, and both cried, neither for bad reasons.

That there was, in fact, a reason his fiancée couldn't ever quite dump him.

That, actually, if you have only had one boyfriend since you were at school, then it's possible, through absolutely nobody's fault, that you have been viewing the world in black and white, and it might take someone else to show you – fairly rigorously – that in fact it was colour all along.

That Maggie had great difficulty walking past Reuben's building for the rest of her life.

If we were to go there.

Chapter Eleven

They were wrapped up in the clean white sheets of the smallest room at Reuben's, which obviously had something like a stag party going on next door, but as it happened, they hadn't slept a wink, so it hadn't bothered them in the slightest. In fact, the noise that was being made next door made them both rather less inhibited than they might have been otherwise.

David was still asleep, Maggie looking cheerfully at the empty champagne bottle lying on the floor, her heart full of astonished gladness.

The room was tiny, but spotlessly clean: scrubbed wooden floors, white sheets and a small balcony looking over the sea and letting the fresh clean air in. It was technically a surf shack, but to Maggie it was the Paris Ritz.

She stared dreamily out of the window for a long time, until she sensed David stirring behind her and turned round, the sheet around her.

'Please take the sheet down,' said David croakily, and she smiled and let it fall.

'You look like Venus with the waves behind you,' he said. 'And Christ, that hair. Come over here, please. Quickly.'

Maggie smiled and went to him gladly. She'd texted Claire telling her not to worry about her, and received a clutch of question marks and exclamation marks in return so had simply turned her phone off. But still, they were only in town. She looked at the beautiful dawning Sunday with some regret; they couldn't walk down the street together. Somebody would see them. Everything would be ruined.

So she decided to ignore the outside world, throw herself into this forbidden sojourn, enjoy every second alone with him.

'Why ... oh, when you never called,' said David, after hunger had finally driven him downstairs, and he'd found that Reuben's stocked the most astonishing bread and sandwiches – really, it was the most peculiar place; he'd never experienced anything like it. And honey with everything, once again. He'd brought it all upstairs and they'd had the most wonderful sticky feast; the fresh air blowing in from the tiny balcony, the noise and chatter of the passers-by below. He'd booked another night, even though they would have to leave this stolen moment sometime; would have to prick the bubble that held them so perfectly.

He'd added a bottle of champagne for good measure.

'I wrote!'

'I didn't get it. I don't ... Oh, it's a long story.'

'But you didn't call, and even when you did, you were so weird ...'

'I thought you were married!'

Maggie shook her head.

'*And* you'd given me the poem ...'

'But ... the poem said everything.'

'It said, *we shall never be friends*!' said Maggie fiercely. 'Oh, I cried and cried.'

David looked confused.

'Yes, and—'

'*All's over,*' said Maggie, looking mutinous. Then she leaned over and kissed him on the nose, because he had, she had decided, a particularly beautiful nose.

'And—'

She shook her head.

'That's it. I didn't read any more. I threw it away, I was so upset. I thought ... I thought you felt bad about it when I saw you.'

David stared at her.

'Is that why ... '

Maggie shrugged.

'I didn't want to get you into trouble.' She looked up at him. 'And I thought you'd be calling me. Though not in the middle of the night.'

'But ... but I thought I'd said everything I needed to say in the poem,' said David ruefully. 'Obviously not.'

He pulled her close to him.

'Oh, the limits of poetry,' he murmured into her scented hair. 'Listen.'

And she laid her head on his shoulder as he recited, slowly:

> '*Shake hands, we shall never be friends, all's over;*
> *I only vex you the more I try.*
> *All's wrong that ever I've done or said,*
> *And nought to help it in this dull head:*
> *Shake hands, here's luck, good-bye.*
>
> *But if you come to a road where danger*
> *Or guilt or anguish or shame's to share,*
> *Be good to the lad that loves you true*
> *And the soul that was born to die for you,*
> *And whistle and I'll be there.*'

Chapter Twelve

Fliss was pleased that Simone was happy again. And, it could not be argued, a little jealous. Yes, obviously, everyone agreed it was absolutely terrible, what a dreadful thing to happen.

But still.

Since Christmas, she and Ismé had hung out almost all the time. Ismé had introduced her to new bands, new ways of dressing and thinking and reading, and she felt she was learning so much about the world she had never really considered in any depth before. She had tried to explain it to her mother over the phone, but her mother had sighed and said was Fliss eating enough and how she really didn't have time as she had to get to something important, which Fliss knew was a hair appointment and her mother said actually, no, it was a charity lunch for the mentally deficient, and Fliss had said crossly that you couldn't say that any more and her mother had said, oh dear, what *could* you say, and then Fliss couldn't remember so it had all been rather awkward.

But it had gone no further – the odd foot rub; Ismé occasionally ruffling Fliss's chic short hair (which her mother was still very much not used to), but not accepting it in return, giving Fliss a fairly stiff lecture about not touching black hair – and Fliss was feeling frustrated and miserable. Which hadn't been helped by Alice and Will obviously being an item again, parading around being romantic. It felt once more like she was the odd one out.

Everyone else was grabbing life with both hands. She'd have to do it too.

Chapter Twelve

Sunday night was heartbreaking. It felt impossible, even though they'd only been together for twenty-four hours, that they could ever be apart again, not for an instant. As if it would break the spell that bound them together.

They talked and talked and talked; poured out how everything had been; what had happened in the time they'd been apart. But neither of them could broach the subject of what to do next.

'You think she'd soften?' said David, meaning Dr Deveral.

'Are you kidding?' said Maggie, wondering seriously if she'd ever wear clothes again. It was just so long since she'd felt . . .

No. She'd *never* felt so happy, so adored; so free in her own skin, in the certain knowledge that for all the faults she could find with it, there was someone who didn't care in the slightest; who thought, in fact (as he truly did), that she was a thing of absolute glory.

'She can't hear your name even now. She's terrified of negative press attention; you know what she's like. And Miss Starling is even worse. God, David, I signed that contract.'

David nodded.

'I see.'

'I could leave,' said Maggie.

'You could come to Phillip Dean with me,' said David.

'Or go back to Scotland.'

David blinked.

'Please don't do that.'

'Okay,' said Maggie. 'But I *will* leave. I'll find something ... move ...'

'Oh God,' said David. 'You're great at that job. They'd be nuts to let you go. There must be a way.'

'If you came back ...' said Maggie shyly.

'That would make everything worse,' said David.

'I know,' said Maggie. 'But at least I'd get to see you.'

'We could sneak out to Reuben's.'

'I've had worse holidays,' said Maggie, smiling.

'But I want to ... I want to go places with you. I want to hold your hand. I want to tell ... I want to tell the world.'

Maggie lay down under his wandering hand, feeling the last rays of the sun hit her.

'Me too.'

She opened her eyes.

'You really wouldn't come back?'

David shrugged his shoulders.

'I think ... I mean. Phillip Dean. It has its problems.'

'I know what you mean,' said Maggie, thinking back to her own old school.

'But I feel I'm making a difference.'

'You make a difference to everyone you meet,' said Maggie gently.

'If I say I feel needed, will you call me horribly conceited and think a lot less of me?'

'Definitely,' said Maggie, pulling him down. 'In fact I must insist that you shut up immediately ...'

Chapter Fourteen

It was as he was driving back – and realising as he did so that even their cars would be a dead giveaway to anyone down in town – that he got the idea. Dr Fitzroy wanted him. The Phillip Dean kids needed better facilities. And he was absolutely desperate to see Maggie; it had been five seconds and he missed her terribly already. For the first time in his life, he wished he knew how a Bluetooth phone worked and that he had one in his car. He just wanted to hear her voice; her laugh, the smile in her voice whenever she turned towards him. He felt like an addict. It was ridiculous.

He did, on the other hand, have an idea.

Chapter Fifteen

Maggie couldn't wait for the following weekend. They'd have to be careful not to be caught, of course – still no phone calls or contact. But somehow that made it even more exciting. She counted down the minutes to Friday night, joyously letting her class off homework now their exams were done and putting up with an incredible amount of nonsense. Even Alice couldn't wind her up, and the girl most certainly tried.

She shaved her legs, washed her hair, said goodbye to Claire (who rolled her eyes, unconvinced) and practically ran to her car.

She wasn't the only one playing hookey. Will, at sixteen, was allowed to stay out in town until 9 p.m. Alice, at fourteen, definitely was not. That was why she was hiding by the laundry, with strict instructions to the others to put two pillows in her bed at lights out and claim she had a headache. Fliss was fairly certain this would never work. Alice was insouciant about it. Simone was in too much of a love dream to be anything other than helpful, however scared she was of Miss Starling, which was quite a lot.

Which was how Alice came to be sitting outside on the terrace at Reuben's when Maggie arrived, listening to Will and his noisy friends talk about rugby and pretending she didn't secretly find it quite dull, seeing as it was pretty exciting to be out in the first place. Her attention wandering, she glanced up . . .

All would have been fine, reflected Maggie, if David, in a fit of absolute joy and excitement, hadn't been standing on the balcony waiting for her, and hadn't waved like a lunatic when he saw her. He'd brought Stephen Dedalus, who woofed excitedly – he'd always adored Maggie – which immediately attracted the attention of everyone in the vicinity, particularly since David had dressed him for the occasion in a particularly natty scarf.

Maggie, below, was helpless with laughter, until she heard the characteristic sound of a camera clicking and turned round. Sitting there laughing hysterically, and in a very fake way, was her teenage nemesis.

Chapter Sixteen

The various options flooded through Maggie's brain, even as David slowly realised what had happened and disappeared back into the room and down the stairs.

Maggie met him at the bottom.

Sod it. Sod the school with its outdated rules. And its silly, rich, entitled girls, and old-time ways and reputations to uphold. Sod it.

She met him full on with a kiss, which surprised him, but in the most delighted way.

'Is there a job for me?' she whispered. 'At Phillip Dean? Because I think I've just been sacked.'

Chapter Seventeen

As they packed their cases, Fliss was still trying to persuade Ismé to come on holiday with her, but Ismé wasn't keen.

'What am I going to do, lie in the sun? I don't think so.'

'Swim?'

'Mmm,' said Ismé, who couldn't swim very well. 'Nah. I have to get back to real life.'

'Do you?' said Fliss. They were in the dorm together. Alice was out with Will again, having come back the previous weekend with a very smug expression and an annoying secret she wouldn't divulge, and Simone was in the library, writing love letters to Ash. 'Do you really?'

She moved closer and, taking a deep breath, put her mouth up to be kissed.

Two things happened at once: firstly, Ismé, after kissing her back to start with, seemed to change her mind and, to Fliss's heartbreak, started to pull away – but not before Alice had marched in, furious.

The marks were up for the exams. Miss Adair's classes had, as usual, done very well. Except for Alice, who had scored exactly as her work deserved: a C–.

Alice had stormed off to Miss Adair's office to complain about her results – she was often persuasive in this way – but

Miss Adair had had none of it, even when Alice threatened to expose what she knew about her and David.

Maggie had grinned.

'Feel free,' she said. 'But Alice, I do think you could be using your undoubted cleverness and talent . . . ' her voice softened, 'to do so much more. To be so much better.'

Alice had stormed out of the office and back to the dorm to complain vociferously, only to find this . . .

Fliss and Ismé leapt apart as Alice rolled her eyes.

'I'll come back, shall I?' she yelled. 'I'm off to request a transfer to Jacobite House. And they're all *awful*.'

The two girls left behind were silent.

'Is . . . '

Ismé shook her head.

'I never led you on.'

'I just . . . I just think you're amazing.'

Ismé stared at the ground.

'Really?'

'Yes. You're different to anyone I've ever met. You're so clever and interesting . . . and you've taught me so much. About everything.'

'But Fliss,' said Ismé, 'all I ever wanted was a friend.'

Chapter Eighteen

Maggie was surprised to see Dr Deveral looking rather flustered on the last day of term. She even had a packed suitcase by her desk. This was very unlike her.

Maggie remembered the last time she'd sat in front of the headmistress, on this very same day last year, terrified to her stomach. And now ... now she was nervous. But in such a different way.

She spoke boldly.

'Dr Deveral ... Veronica,' she said. 'I have to tell you something.'

Veronica nodded, distracted.

'Yes, yes, I know, Dr Fitzroy phoned me. You want to leave.'

'I don't want to,' said Maggie, realising she was sounding rather more formal than she might have. 'I don't want to leave at all. I love the school.'

She did, she realised. Despite the occasional Alice. It was her home.

'But I have to. You know why.'

Dr Deveral heaved a great sigh.

'Oh for heaven's sake.'

She moved some papers on her desk.

'Dr Fitzroy wants him back. And now you want to go.'

'We want to be together,' said Maggie, aware that she sounded ridiculous and rather wishing she'd brought David with her. But that would have felt very wrong.

'I know, I know . . . Ah, here it is.'

'What's that?'

Maggie squinted at the paper.

'Intake exchange. I was just thinking . . . Some of our girls – Alice Trebizon-Woods springs to mind – are very narrow in their thinking. And some of our scholarship girls and boys are having trouble fitting in. So. From next year we're going to run an exchange scheme. With one of the local schools.'

Maggie blinked.

'Phillip Dean?'

'Phillip Dean. Do you think you could go . . . on exchange there for a term?'

Maggie clasped her hands together.

'A term?'

Dr Deveral peered over her glasses.

'I assume you'll know what you want after a term. And then . . . I'm sure everything will be fine.'

'Oh my . . . oh my goodness. Thank you!'

'Thank Mr McDonald. It's his idea. He's going to be liaison.'

Maggie's grin threatened to crack her face.

'That's . . . that's just wonderful.'

'Now. Off you go. Enjoy your summer.'

David had promised to take her down the Amalfi coast. Maggie couldn't wait.

'I shall.'

She frowned as the main door buzzed.

'Who is that?'

Dr Deveral jumped up, startled.

'No one,' she said, abruptly. 'Now, shoo . . .'

As Maggie lingered on the staircase, she caught a

glimpse of a tall, stooped man with a vast mop of very white hair, a booming voice and a thick accent she didn't quite recognise, before the door to Veronica's office was firmly shut.

Chapter Nineteen

Ismé's mum held onto her like she wouldn't ever let her go.

'My darling girl,' she said, burying her head in her hair. 'I missed you so much.'

'You too, Mum,' said Ismé.

'Tell me it wasn't too awful.'

Ismé held out her report card. There it was, in black and white. A grades in every subject.

Her mother hugged her again.

'You are never going to have to do what I do,' she whispered in her daughter's ear, and Ismé closed her eyes and reminded herself she was going to have to grin and bear it after all.

'And the girls are good girls?' her mother asked. 'Not too much sex and drugs and rock and roll?'

Ismé smiled at the old-fashioned language.

'Well,' she said, 'I don't know what rock and roll is, and there aren't many drugs. Don't ask me about the other thing.'

Her mother rolled her eyes and followed her into the flat.

Chapter Twenty

Ashok's father and Simone's parents had waited as long as they reasonably could, but this goodbye was getting very awkward. Simone had grown even more, it seemed, and Ash looked tiny, but they were hugging as if they were being separated for ever.

'So, ahem,' tried Simone's mother.

Both sets of parents were feeling extremely awkward.

'You live in London?'

'Southgate.'

'Enfield!' said Simone's mother. 'We're practically neighbours!'

All three shuffled their feet.

'Come on, Ashok!' shouted his father for the fourth time.

'Perhaps . . . ' Simone's dad said, looking at his daughter's happy face as the tiny boy headed off, 'perhaps you could visit in the holidays.'

'She needs to work,' hissed Simone's mother, but her father shushed her. 'I'm sure we can find some time. Everyone needs to relax.'

Simone beamed through her tears, and didn't fall out with her brother once on the long journey home.

Chapter Twenty-one

Maggie put on a big hat as they drove to the ferry, even though the sky was overcast and rain threatened, and David laughed at her as she added huge sunglasses. She took out her book and pretended to ignore him, and he put some Elbow on his old CD player in the car and they turned it up loudly, and she was the happiest person in the world even as her telephone rang.

'Hello? Hello?'

At first she couldn't hear who it was, and she couldn't read it through her dark glasses. Then she recognised her sister's voice.

'Anne? Anne? What is it?'

'Look. Something's happened.'

'What? Is it Cody or Dylan?'

David shot her a look and turned the CD player off. The rain started to pound against the roof of the little car.

'No,' said Anne, her voice choking. 'It's Stan.'

Acknowledgements

Thanks first off to the two Jos: Jo Unwin, and Jo Dickinson who never lost the faith with *Class*. It still remains the only book I have ever been interrogated about by sales reps. ☺ And Maddie West, who was equally keen to revive it: thank you.

Deborah Schneider, who probably won't even remember how encouraging she was about this series, but it meant a lot to me. Charlie King, David Shelley, Joanna Kramer, Viola Hayden, Stephie Melrose, Gemma Shelley and the whole team at Little, Brown.

Everyone who wrote, tweeted or facebooked me to (some times quite crossly) demand to know what on earth was happening to Maggie and David, and could they possibly find out before we were all dead: I wouldn't, and couldn't, have done it without you.

Also I need to thank Sean Kemp, who answered a question about Downing Street for me in a previous book but I forgot to thank him in that one. Cheers.

~ DREAM WITH ~

JENNY COLGAN

Keep in touch with Jenny and her readers:

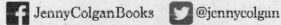
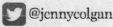 JennyColganBooks @jennycolgan

JennyColganBooks

Check out Jenny's website and sign up to her newsletter for all the latest book news plus mouth-watering recipes.

www.jennycolgan.com

LOVE TO READ?

Join **The Little Book Café** for competitions, sneak peeks and more.

 TheLittleBookCafe   @littlebookcafe

An unmissable series from *Sunday Times* bestseller JENNY COLGAN

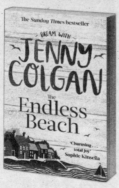

Escape to the Scottish Isle of Mure, an idyllic and quirky place where friends Lorna and Flora search for their happy ever after.

'Charming, made me long to escape to Mure. Total joy'
SOPHIE KINSELLA

'Gorgeous, glorious, uplifting'
MARIAN KEYES

Life is sweet!

As the cobbled alleyways of Paris come to life, Anna Trent is already at work, mixing and stirring the finest chocolate. It's a huge shift from the chocolate factory she used to work in back home until an accident changed everything. With old wounds about to be uncovered and healed, Anna is set to discover more about real chocolate – and herself – than she ever dreamed.

Can baking mend a broken heart?

Polly Waterford is recovering from a toxic relationship. Unable to afford their flat, she has to move to a quiet seaside resort in Cornwall, where she lives alone. And so Polly takes out her frustrations on her favourite hobby: making bread. With nuts and seeds, olives and chorizo, and with reserves of determination Polly never knew she had, she bakes and bakes and bakes. And people start to hear about it ...

'Sheer indulgence from start to finish'
SOPHIE KINSELLA

Meet Issy Randall, proud owner of the Cupcake Café

After a childhood spent in her beloved Grampa Joe's bakery, Issy Randall has undoubtedly inherited his talent, so when she's made redundant from her job, Issy decides to seize the moment. Armed with recipes from Grampa, the Cupcake Café opens its doors. But Issy has absolutely no idea what she's let herself in for . . .

One way or another, Issy is determined to have a merry Christmas!

Issy Randall is in love and couldn't be happier. Her new business is thriving and she is surrounded by close friends. But when her boyfriend is scouted for a possible move to New York, Issy is forced to face up to the prospect of a long-distance romance, and she must decide what she holds most dear.

'An evocative, sweet treat'
JOJO MOYES

Remember the rustle of the pink and green striped paper bag?

Rosie Hopkins thinks leaving her busy London life and her boyfriend, Gerard, to sort out her elderly Aunt Lilian's sweetshop in a small country village is going to be dull. Boy, is she wrong. Lilian Hopkins has spent her life running Lipton's sweetshop, through wartime and family feuds. As she struggles with the idea that it might finally be time to settle up, she also wrestles with the secret history hidden behind the jars of beautifully coloured sweets.

Curl up with Rosie, her friends and her family as they prepare for a very special Christmas...

Rosie is looking forward to Christmas. Her sweetshop is festooned with striped candy canes, large tempting piles of Turkish Delight, crinkling selection boxes and happy, sticky children. She's going to be spending it with her boyfriend, Stephen, and her family, flying in from Australia. She can't wait. But when a tragedy strikes at the heart of their little community, all of Rosie's plans are blown apart. Is what's best for the sweetshop also what's best for Rosie?

'A fun, warm-hearted read'
WOMAN & HOME

There's more than one surprise in store for Rosie Hopkins this Christmas...

Rosie Hopkins, newly engaged, is looking forward to an exciting year in the little sweetshop she owns and runs. But when fate strikes Rosie and her boyfriend, Stephen, a terrible blow, threatening everything they hold dear, it's going to take all their strength and the support of their families and their Lipton friends to hold them together.

After all, don't they say it takes a village to raise a child?

Meet Nina

Given a back-room computer job when the beloved Birmingham library she works in turns into a downsized retail complex, Nina misses her old role terribly – dealing with people, greeting her regulars and making sure everyone gets the right books for their needs. Then a new business nobody else wants catches her eye: owning a tiny little bookshop bus up in the Scottish highlands. Out all hours in the freezing cold, driving with a tiny stock of books ... can Nina really make it work?

'A natural, funny, warm-hearted writer'
LISA JEWELL

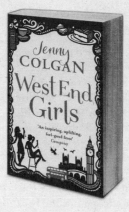

The streets of London are the perfect place to discover your dreams…

When, out of the blue, twin sisters Lizzie and Penny learn they have a grandmother living in Chelsea, they are even more surprised when she asks them to flat-sit her King's Road pad while she is in hospital. They jump at the chance to move to London but, as they soon discover, it's not easy to become an It Girl, and West End boys aren't at all like Hugh Grant …

Sun, sea and laughter abound in this warm, bubbly tale

Evie is desperate for a good holiday with peaceful beaches, glorious sunshine and (fingers crossed) some much-needed sex. So when her employers invite her to attend a conference in the beautiful South of France, she can't believe her luck. At last, the chance to party under the stars with the rich and glamorous, to live life as she'd always dreamt of it. But things don't happen in quite the way Evie imagines …

> ‘Colgan at her warm,
> down-to-earth best’
> *COSMOPOLITAN*

How does an It Girl survive when she loses everything?

Sophie Chesterton is a girl about town, but deep down she suspects that her superficial lifestyle doesn't amount to very much. Her father is desperate for her to make her own way in the world, and when after one shocking evening her life is turned upside down, she suddenly has no choice. Barely scraping by, living in a hovel with four smelly boys, eating baked beans from the tin, Sophie is desperate to get her life back. But does a girl really need diamonds to be happy?

A feisty, flirty tale of one woman's quest to cure her disastrous love life

Posy is delighted when Matt proposes, but a few days later disaster strikes: he backs out of the engagement. Crushed and humiliated, Posy wonders why her love life has always ended in disaster. Determined to discover how she got to this point, Posy resolves to get online and track down her exes. Can she learn from past mistakes? And what if she has let Mr Right slip through her fingers on the way?

~ DREAM WITH ~

JENNY COLGAN

writing as Jenny T. Colgan in

LOCAL GIRL SWEPT OFF HER FEET

Mild-mannered publicist Holly Phillips is unlucky in love.
She's embarrassed beyond belief when the handsome stranger she
meets in a bar turns out to be 'Ultimate Man' – a superpowered hero
whose rescue attempt finds her hoisted over his shoulder and flashing
her knickers in the newspaper the next day.

But when Holly's fifteen minutes of fame make her a target for something
villainous, she only has one place to turn – and finds the man behind the
mask holds a lot more charm than his crime-fighting alter-ego.

**Can Holly find love, or is superdating just as complicated
as the regular kind?**